YEAR OF THE QUEEN

Jeremy Stanford

Tale

First published in Australia by Wild and Woolley Press 2007

Reprinted by BPA Print Group.
Republished by Tale Publishing
https://talepublishing.com/

Cover design by Anne-Marie Reeves.
Edited by Kathryn Moore.

Cover photograph kindly provided by Priscilla on Stage.
Cover outfit designed and created by Lizzy Gardiner and Tim
Chappel.
Photograph 1, reproduced with kind permission from David
Spencer.
Photographs 3, 6 & 7 reproduced with kind permission from
Michael Caton.

National Library of Australia Cataloguing-in-Publication entry:
Creator: Stanford, Jeremy, author.
Title: Year of the Queen / Jeremy Stanford.
ISBN: 978-0-9944399-8-7 (paperback)
Subjects: Biography and Memoir.

Contacts:
Lisa Mann, C/O Lisa Mann Creative Management.
lisa@lmcm.com.au
Direct: year.of.thequeen@hotmail.com

This book is dedicated to my angel, Annie,
and my two best mates, Hunter and Ned.
And in loving memory of a true genius
of the theatre and a dear friend,
Ross Coleman

Elvis

I feel like death warmed up. I've collapsed across a corduroy sofa in the pastel surrounds of a city hotel. My head throbs, my joints ache, and I'm coughing up ghastly hunks of green phlegm. It's Friday afternoon, and in just three hours I'm supposed to be on stage for the final preview of *Priscilla, Queen of the Desert — The Musical.* Tomorrow night is the much touted 'world premiere'.

After an eight year break from big musical theatre, I've been honoured with the dizzying responsibility of playing one of the three leads—an act of unbelievable good faith, which I am determined to repay—but right now I haven't got a clue how I'm going to get through it. I just want it all to go away.

I stare vacantly at the alarming collection of pills, potions, and antibiotics assembled across the glass-topped coffee table, none of which have delivered the aid promised on the labels. I've been firing this growing arsenal of remedies across the bow of my illness for a week now, but nothing's worked. I've tried everything imaginable, have even seen a hypnotist, but it's all been nothing more than passing foliage along the highway to hell.

Out of desperation, I've committed what's deemed to be a mortal sin in the theatre: I've turned off my mobile phone and holed up in this hotel room as though I'm Elvis, so there'll be no chance they can draw me back into the chaotic nightmare that's going on backstage. A torturous three weeks has ground me into a paste, and I've finally accepted that I've run out of ideas of how to make it across the finish line. I implore a higher power to intervene and somehow bring me salvation.

A mysterious impulse makes me reach for my phone and switch it on. Seconds after it boots up, like magic, it rings. Is this the sign I've beseeched? Am I saved?

'Hello?' I croak.

'Jeremy?'

It's Sandra, our company manager. Her voice is both alarmed and concerned.

'I think I've got something here that might help you.'

Chapter 1
When the Phone Rang
Christmas 2005

Who'd be an actor, huh? I call it a high wire act—others call it 'that thing you do between waiting tables'. To keep yourself from pouring lattes your entire life, you need the cunning of a gutter rat, lashings of faith and a darn good sense of humour. It pays to be versatile, so life becomes a patchwork quilt of varying jobs, their threads overlapping and interweaving, ultimately keeping everything in place.

Here's a snapshot of what's on the slate and keeps my world turning circa Christmas 2005: I've been commissioned to write a feature film, I'm script editing another, I'm directing a music video, playing bass guitar in two bands, working part-time as a casting director, and doing voice-over work and corporate theatre. The last full time salary I made as an actor was a Playbox play, back in September 2004. My life is complex and diverse to say the least.

When the phone rings with the offer to be part of the workshop for *Priscilla*, I've just finished pitching the feature film I've been script editing, and I'm on my way to read the eulogy at a friend's funeral. I've struggled to get out the door in the first place as my wife, Annie, who's also a performer, is singing Christmas carols in a trio called *The Holly Belles*, and there's a potential crossover with the kids. Serious juggling is going on. If I don't get home in time, Hunter, five, and Ned, two, could be left standing like bewildered, unloved calves in the street, mooing to the horizon for their parents.

I make my meeting, and the producer I'm pitching to is cautiously positive about the script. As the writer and I descend the soaring city skyscraper trying to interpret what he's just said to us, my guts are churning, half from the despair of having to read the eulogy in forty minutes, and half from the excitement that, finally, a producer seems interested in one of my film projects.

In 1999, after nearly twenty years as an actor, I'd had the sudden brainwave to go to film school. Like a madman, I'd decided to leave behind the insecurity of an acting life and retrain, move on to something with some real job security: film directing! Six years on and my journey has brought me to this point. As I sift through the fragments of our meeting, I'm not even really sure where that is.

We hit the street and my phone rings. A familiar warm current of expectation runs through me as the caller I.D. tells me it's my agent. Any actor will tell you that the moment you see your agent calling feels like being back at the lucky dip at your best friend's birthday party when you were five. What could this be? A badly paid ad for incontinence, Baz Luhrmann has finally seen my brilliant work on *Blue Heelers* and wants me for his latest blockbuster, or the accounts department wants those tax forms back?

I farewell the writer and take the call. I'm sheltering from the searing December sun in my funeral suit as my agent, Lisa, asks what I'm up to in January. I'm sprung. I should have mentioned a little workshop I'm doing for a musical called *Three And a Half*, about a martian who's crash landed on earth and wants to get home. It was a cash job—so no commission necessary—and I hadn't said anything because the money was crap, and January is notoriously quiet. No one works in January. Only David Wenham. She would never have found out.

'January?' I say nervously, but with expectation. 'Not much.'

She tells me about *Priscilla*. A bunch of producers have bought the rights to put it on stage as a musical. It's workshopping for ten days with a studio performance at the end to see if the idea has legs. She doesn't know who the producers are, only that it's at the Melbourne Theatre Company Rehearsal Studios, but has nothing to do with the Melbourne Theatre Company. They've asked if I'd like to play Tick, the Hugo Weaving role.

This is like a light bulb going on. It instantly makes sense. Of all films to convert into a musical this one was perfect, and I could picture myself playing the role.

What was going on? I'd be working in January!

Lisa trots out the workshopping dates, and of course they clash with *Three And a Half*. Story of my life. I'll have to fess up about the other job. You'd think I'd be safe to conceal a little job like this from my agent, but suddenly January is filling up. Who am I, David fucking Wenham?

Priscilla turns out to be a way better offer than *Three And a Half*. For a start, the script for *Three And a Half* needs major surgery, not just a workshop, the money's lousy, and they've already said it's highly unlikely to go in to production in the foreseeable future. The problem is that I've already committed to it.

I tell Lisa I'm extremely interested in *Priscilla*, but I have to talk to the director of the other show first. I won't pull out if they feel they can't replace me.

Babs McMillan is the director in question. She's the reason I've committed to the workshop in the first place.

She's complete theatre royalty, and I adore her. The irony strikes me that it's really because of Babs I've been offered the job in *Priscilla*. She's responsible for getting me into musical theatre.

Back in 1991, I'd auditioned for a Playbox play she was directing. She'd seemed completely detached through the whole audition until the end, when she'd asked if I played guitar.

'Of course,' I'd said, hoping that answer would get me the job.

It didn't, but a couple of weeks later my agent rang—familiar warm current of expectation—and asked if I'd like to audition for the title role in *The Buddy Holly Story*. The show had already been running in Sydney for about four months, with an imported Brit playing the role, but now Babs was at the helm she was looking for an Australian to take over.

I auditioned for Babs, and then they flew me to Sydney to audition for the producer. The show was playing at Her Majesty's Theatre, and I was escorted to the bowels of the theatre to meet the production team. They were extremely effusive when I arrived. They even had my actor's headshot on their desk with Buddy Holly glasses drawn on my face in Texta. They were extremely warm and welcoming. I call it *the shine*. It's that feeling when you know you're the one they like for the role. You do your audition and the director immediately bonds with you because they know they're going to be working with you soon. It's palpable when you get it, but it's also crystal clear when you don't. Directors can be as sweet and complimentary about your work as they like, but when you don't get *the shine,* you don't get the job.

I did my audition for the producer, and I got the job. It was the biggest break I'd had in my career, and it set me up for about ten years straight of work in musical theatre. I also got a wife out of the bargain. In the second incarnation of the show, Annie joined the cast, and I instantly fell in love with this unbelievably gorgeous and talented Kiwi. By the third incarnation, we were married and playing husband and wife *as* husband and wife. Touring through Australia and New Zealand with the show was a kind of working honeymoon. Not only was it a publicist's dream come true, it was ours as well.

So now, after helping me achieve all that, here I am, a squeaking little rodent, trying to weasel my way out of Babs' workshop. I call and run *Priscilla* past her. She insists I do it, thank God. The one thing you can count on with true bastions of the theatrical world is that they look after each other. She can sniff the potential for me and lets me go like a fairy thistle into the wind.

The year is hurtling towards Christmas. Once the funeral is over, I feel like I can put 2005 back in the rack. Annie, the kids, and I are about to head off for a freezing, wet Melbourne Christmas at Point Lonsdale. There's a lot to like about 2006: a music video to direct, a film to write, and a workshop about drag queens in the desert.

The patchwork quilt that will be 2006 seems enticing. There are a lot of frayed ends to be tidied and sorted, but I'm liking the design.

Chapter 2
A Toe in the Water
The first workshop, Jan 23rd – 1st Feb

Since our return from Point Lonsdale, I've been writing the film script. Ideas bubbled away as we shivered through freezing days on the beach, and the script took shape in my mind. Now, it seems to be writing itself. I've shot the video clip I've been working on, and have been trying to edit it, but my computer hasn't been behaving since it was struck by lightning on Christmas Eve.

As the *Priscilla* workshop approaches, I've pretty much finished the first draft of the script. I'm not going to send it through to the producer just yet. Having the ten days away from it will give me some much-needed perspective, and I don't want to send her a pile of poop. I'll pretend I'm still writing it, while I'm away on secondment to *Priscilla*. It'll make it seem like it's taken me longer to write. I don't want the producer to think it was too easy.

There's been a trickle of gossip coming through about the workshop. The producers are Back Row Productions, a mob from Britain who made their money from Dein

Perry's *Tap Dogs*, amongst other things. Simon Phillips will be directing.

Simon is the artistic director of the Melbourne Theatre Company (MTC) and is a bit of a scatty genius, who famously wears odd socks and no shoes when he's working. He defies what someone in his position should be like. For a start, you'd imagine someone older, a brooding, remote, theatrical giant—at the very least someone more cut throat. But Simon is boyish and charming and has risen to his position so quickly by being a rare talent, and an ultimately capable wunderkind. He's Mr Likeable. Every actress in the country has a crush on him. He has the face of a man ten years his junior, though he often wears the fatigue of his long working hours. He's enthusiastic, generous, and hilarious to work with. Simon's rehearsal periods are famous for being a riot. Despite the madness, somehow the work still gets done. I'm constantly fascinated by him when we work together because he simultaneously keeps the work progressing and engenders a cheerful working environment. I first worked with him on *High Society*, back in 1993, and then again on *Company*, in 2000.

Ross Coleman is choreographing. Simon and Ross pretty much come as a team. Ross choreographed *High Society*, and many more of Simon's productions. He's one of the most talented people I've ever met. He seems to conjure his choreography from thin air, never having prepared anything before he begins. People heap praise on him, which he shrinks from. But if he feels overlooked he'll turn like a cut snake. Where other 'theatrical' types are flamboyant, Ross prides himself on being plain reprehensible. He delights in recounting extraordinary, head spinning tales, just to watch your reaction. He betrays a slightly wicked glint as he tells these stories, to remind you that the reservoir from which this little tit-bit came is vast enough to completely fry your brain.

Aside from being a wonderful choreographer, Ross

lives to cook. He regularly expounds on his most recent accomplishments with goat or duck, and once wearily remarked that his Russian partner, Oleg, had unexpectedly arrived home from the market with a hare, and *what was he to do with it!* He lives around the corner from me, and I often bump into him. Late one night I snuck out to get some milk and found Ross and Oleg strolling down the street, glass of shiraz in hand, hunting for some fresh bay leaves to pick for their evening meal.

Annie and I stayed with them in East Berlin when Ross was choreographing at the Friedrichstadt-Palast.

When we arrived, Oleg was cooking pork, so we nicked off to the bottle shop to stock up for the night. Ross went around grabbing armfuls of liquor, packing them into brown paper bags. Once back at the apartment we started on the vodka, and we drank toasts until that bottle ran out. Oleg had been boiling the hock of pork for about two hours at that stage. Then he took it out and put it into the oven, and we started on the red wine. After the second bottle, Oleg finally pulled the pork out of the oven and began to look like serving it. Hours had passed. Annie and I hadn't eaten since midday, and it was now eleven thirty at night. The smell of the pork was out of control, but the torture wasn't over yet. Oleg had to crisp the roasted veggies. That next half hour seemed to drag on for an eternity as I tried to focus through dizzying spells of drunkenness.

Finally the pork was served, and I ate it like a mad dog. It was *the* most delicious thing I had ever eaten— incredible.

Now, when Ross talks about the meals he and Oleg create, there's a part of me that feels like I have Stockholm syndrome. It felt like torture, that night in East Berlin, having to wait like some kind of prisoner for those incredible smells coming from the oven to convert into actual food. When I hear about his latest culinary masterpiece I want to be back in East Berlin, deliriously drunk, wrestling with my desperate hunger, only to be rewarded with culinary perfection. I want to feel the delicious agony once more.

Aside from Ross and Simon, the rest of the personnel for the workshop are a mystery. On our first morning I call Ross to offer him a lift to the MTC. It's not quite a selfless act. This way I can drill him for any gossip he might have about the show. When he gets into the car he waves my question away saying no one tells him anything. He does know that Spud Murphy is the musical director. He says until the last few days they didn't have anyone to fill the job, so Ross called Spud to bring him on board. They'd worked together on *Dusty*, and he's apparently fabulous with musical arrangements.

We enter the cavernous rehearsal room at the MTC. Everything in the room exists on an enormous scale. You push through huge doors to an open expanse of raw floorboards and soaring, canvas-draped walls, and instantly you feel dusty. The room is centred around a long meeting table, which is groaning with scripts and song books.

A few cast members have already gathered. Nicki Wendt, a blonde bombshell who I've worked with many times before, is playing my wife. We piss ourselves laughing when she dryly quips, 'Finally, I get to play your wife and you're a poof!'

Other actors straggle in. John Wood is playing Bob. Spencer McLaren is playing Felicia, the Guy Pearce role. Colette Mann and D.J. Foster arrive not knowing who the hell they're playing.

It's very exciting. No one has the slightest idea of what we'll be doing or who is involved, so the surprises keep coming.

Tony Sheldon arrives. He's playing Bernadette, the Terence Stamp role. Tony is a man who can fill a room. People seem to erupt around him like Rotorua geysers. He's so loved, and it's easy to see why. When you're with him he makes you feel like no one else exists. He shines his generous light on you, and you seem to grow like Jack's beanstalk. He still fills me with awe from having seen his astounding performance in *Torch Song Trilogy* twenty years ago. I introduce myself, working on the assumption that he may not remember me. He scoffs at my humility. We have a quick chat, and he's stolen away by someone else, eager for his attention.

Spud arrives. He has a no-nonsense look about him and seems like he just wants to get cracking.

We assemble around the table and scripts, and roles are assigned. Simon introduces everyone by way of gently taking the piss out of them. It's his way of breaking the ice. Allan Scott, one of the producers and co-writer of the script, is at one end of the table with his female assistant, who is gorgeous and half his age. Simon introduces them by telling us they have travelled from London together to be here. He leans heavily on the assurance that *nothing untoward is going on between them.* Everyone laughs. Stephan Elliot, the writer and director of the film sits conspicuously at the opposite end of the table from Allan. Allan has a great deal of pedigree, having written the acclaimed film, *Don't Look Now,* which won an Oscar, but this doesn't change the fact that there seems to be an icy breeze blowing between him and Stephan. A story I've heard is that Stephan was reluctant to come on board the project because he didn't believe it could work on stage.

Stephan also seems to have laboured under the guilt of having stolen several people's life stories to write *Priscilla.* Sydney has an infamous transsexual named Carlotta, who the character of Bernadette is based on. She apparently feels exploited by the film—that a lot of people, except her, became rich and famous telling her story. There is also a real life Tick, who is a drag queen and a father. Stephan, in his vision for the stage production of *Priscilla,* wanted to right these wrongs. Before we begin our read, Simon explains this to us. He says that the script incorporates a tribute to Carlotta, and that it was her story portrayed in the film. Apparently, there was talk of her playing herself in the show at one stage, but the idea was quickly abandoned.

Simon explains the origins of the script. Stephan had presented Allan with a draft that depicted a bunch of actors trying to stage a version of *Priscilla, Queen of the Desert*. Only the 'behind the scenes' action would be shown, and none of the story of *Priscilla*. It was all about the real life actors and characters of the drag subculture in Sydney. I get the feeling Allan had a minor coronary when he read it. He'd been handed a musical about *Priscilla* without any *Priscilla* in it. Who'd go to see *that*? Allan then had a crack at the script and put some of the film story back into it. Thus, in the second draft there was a backstory: three actors and a director try to stage the musical of *Priscilla*, and a front story: the actual show, *Priscilla*. Where the two men stand with the current version of the script is not clear, but they don't appear to be high-fiving each other.

Stephan remains unconvinced that the show can work on stage. It was a road movie. How do you put that on stage? The producers seem unsure as well, and the goal of this workshop is to have a good rattle of the script and see if there's anything in this idea that would make a good musical.

We begin the read.

The play opens with a young director pitching a musical based on a famous film to a group of producers. The scene oozes cynicism. I get the feeling that pitching to hard-arsed producers is something Stephan is familiar with. In the play, the producers tell him he's wasting his time; it'll never work. He lists a number of alternatives that could work on stage, but the producers reject them. He finally comes up with *Priscilla*, and to his delight it's accepted. The director tracks down the original people the film is based on and convinces them to be in the show.

They start to rehearse, and this is when we see some of the *Priscilla* story.

As the script continues, the real life story starts to interweave with the show story. The director turns out to be the estranged real life son of the actor playing Tick, so the actor playing Tick is discovering his son, at the same time as the character Tick is discovering *his* son. Sound complex? Yup! At times during the read I begin to read a line and have to stop halfway through because I can't work out which character I'm supposed to be playing. Because both my character and my character's character have sons, I can't work out which son is talking to which character.

All the readers are struggling to keep up with what on earth is going on, who is who, and what they're supposed to be playing.

Stephan's mood worsens as we continue. He sits through the entire read with a face like a slapped bum. He looks like he's going to stand up and scream, "STOP!" It's incredibly hard to act when you can palpably feel the director of this wonderful film hating every moment of what he's hearing.

When we finally limp to the end of the read, a deathly silence falls over the table. We look up from our scripts. No one can find words. Stephan stands up stiffly, leans into Simon's ear, whispers something and then storms out. Simon waits for the huge door to close behind Stephan, before he turns to us and draws a long breath. Finally, he says, 'I think we should take a break,' and heads towards Allan.

The actors sit quietly, still stunned. Colette Mann pipes up with a little voice and says, 'Was it just me, or was anyone else completely confused?' This opens the floodgates. Suddenly we're an angry mob, turning on the script. There's a sense of utter shock amongst us at how confusing and terrible it is.

We go out to the MTC café for morning tea. There's

an overwhelming feeling that we'll all be going home very, very shortly. Whatever Stephan whispered to Simon, it probably spelt doom for the workshop and the entire project. This flirtation with staging a musical of *Priscilla* may well be torpedoed by the time we get back from morning tea. They'll cut their losses, pay us a cancellation fee, and get back on the plane for London.

Taking an iconic movie, which our country and the rest of the world took to its heart, and then adapting it to the stage, complete with musical numbers, is after all risky and ballsy. How do you adapt a road movie set on a bus to the stage? How do you recreate performances by huge Hollywood stars like Hugo Weaving, Guy Pearce and Terence Stamp? The enormity of it hits me as we sit waiting for the verdict.

When we're called back into the rehearsal room, Simon looks grave. We wait for our marching orders with a sense of the inevitable. Stephan is nowhere to be seen, but the rest of the creative team, and the producers, are still here.

Simon very diplomatically announces that what we've just read was an idea the writers wanted to try, which clearly didn't work. A grimacing agreement ripples around the table. Then he confides that what Stephan whispered to him was that we should abandon the script he'd written and go back to the story of the film.

Simon offers us a projected plan for how to attack the rest of the workshop. We'll start at the beginning of the film notating the scenes one by one, and we'll put them on their feet. As we go we'll be throwing in ideas for songs. There are plenty in the film already, but the plan is to source more, which the characters can sing to further the narrative. Once we've learned the songs, Ross will choreograph them. Next Wednesday, the rest of the producers and other potential creatives will come to see what we've come up with.

I'm relieved we're not going home. I like the plan, but I seriously doubt we'll get through the entire show in the limited time we've got.

First we're asked to decide whether the best formula for the show is a "Jukebox Musical" (making all the songs covers), or whether we should commission a composer to write them. The overwhelming consensus is the former. Since so much of the feel of the film is about the seventies and eighties music, it would be a crime to replace these disco classics with new, original songs.

We start with music while the first of the scenes is notated and printed off. We sit in front of a whiteboard and begin to brainstorm songs we could use in the show. They need to be seventies or eighties disco type songs. The first place we need to put one is in the funeral scene, where Bernadette is burying her partner, Trumpet. We all throw in suggestions, and it immediately becomes competitive. Everyone wants to make their mark and get a song in the show. After a hilarious brainstorming session, the winning song is chosen: 'Don't Leave Me This Way', by Donna Summer. This is Ross Coleman's idea. It was the song played at Richard Wherrett's funeral. When his suggestion gets the nod, he roars like he's won the lottery.

The next song is the one that introduces Felicia. We need something rocky for him to perform as a macho 'now' drag queen. Suggestions fly, but John Wood scores with 'Simply Irresistible', by Robert Palmer.

And on it goes. Once we've chosen a few songs, we gather around the piano and begin with 'Don't Leave Me This Way'. Spud creates harmonies out of thin air, and we learn them. Then we hit the floor, and Ross begins to choreograph it. Before we know it, the whole number is choreographed and we can show Simon what we've done. It's exhilarating.

Pages of dialogue arrive, and Simon begins staging the start of the show. Scripts in hand, we plot a simple blocking (a roadmap for where the actors should move on stage) for the opening, where Tick takes a phone call from his wife in Alice Springs, and she demands he come up and see his son. He then rings Bernadette to invite her to join him, but finds her in tears over the death of her boyfriend. We add these scenes to the dance routine, and in seemingly no time we've got the first five minutes of the show done. Steps are wobbly, harmonies are uncertain, and scripts are flapping everywhere, but it cracks along nicely, and everyone is thrilled. We break for the day feeling elated.

Tuesday. Simon brings in new pages. He's clearly been up all night transcribing scenes from the film. As they're printing, we sing through more songs. Today we'll look at the scene directly after the funeral where Tick asks Bernadette to come to Alice Springs with him. While we do this, Spencer and some dancers choreograph 'Simply Irresistible' with Ross. The workshop feels like it's stepped up a gear. People are scattered throughout the building working on scenes or songs, scripts are being edited and printed off, scenes are nipped and tucked and then either thrown out or kept, songs are sourced online, and sheet music is chased down.

We put 'Simply Irresistible' into Felicia's introduction scene, then we block the scene into 'Go West', which brings the bus on stage. We use a taped version of the Pet Shop Boys song to choreograph to. Ross provides some basic moves, and in what seems like no time at all, we've got another five to ten minutes of the show. We're now up to the scene where the drags leave Sydney. It's dizzying how fast the process is moving. To finish the day we mock up the start of the show—where I mime 'I've Never Been To Me'—and we continue through the rest of what we've put together. It's shambolic and uncertain, but everyone has a real crack at it. There's a group feeling that what we're creating could really work.

As the performance approaches, I begin to realise how many bigwigs will be watching on the day. The thought crosses my mind that I'd really like to be in it, should the show get the go-ahead. Would they use me, or go with someone with a bigger profile? Regardless, I'm keen to do the best job I can and not drop my pants in front of a bunch of theatrical luminaries. I'm working hard at nailing this.

I've started prioritising what is important for putting together a decent performance for the showing. First thing is to get my nose out of the script. I can learn lines quite quickly, so I make sure I get the book down on each scene as we do it. The problem is that things change so quickly in a process like this. No sooner have you learnt a scene than it's cut or changed somehow, and you have to learn the new version, and then the new, new version.

I decide to create a little choreography for myself for 'I've Never Been To Me', because when I did it the first time I felt incredibly exposed and uncomfortable miming it. Why wouldn't I? I'm standing in a huge rehearsal room with no wig, make-up or dress, miming a song as a woman. Ross is too busy to do it, so I resolve to do it myself at home.

Spud and Simon take me away to try out a song for the moment when Tick mourns never having been there for his son. The song we've come up with is 'Lullaby', by Billy Joel. It's hauntingly beautiful. I've never heard it before, so I read the sheet music over Spud's shoulder as he plays. My voice is rusty. I haven't sung for two years, and I recognise this as something I really have to get together for the performance. I know if I sing this song well it could be a beautiful moment in the show.

At home that night, I start choreographing 'I've Never Been To Me', and revising lines and song lyrics. The weekend is fast approaching, and the show isn't anywhere near finished. Each time we go back to the top of the show, it's like we've never done it before. Parts of it are decent, but then we get to places where we're all just running around like a bunch of headless chooks. Sometimes the run stops completely because we're all busy laughing at how crap we are.

Saturday. We do a run of what we have so far. We get up to me singing 'Lullaby'. I've worked on the song, but it's still not there yet. I'm not even certain of the tune, and I totally mangle it. As much as this is just a workshop, when something goes badly like that you feel like the worst actor to ever walk the earth. I leave for the day, hanging my head.

Monday. The cast drag themselves in from the weekend. Simon clearly hasn't rested, and there's a pile of new scripts being handed out. Half the Tasmanian old-growth forest is scattered around the room, and people scramble through piles of pages trying to sort out which is the latest version of the script. The race is now on to get to Wednesday.

Everyone is being completely proactive. Tony, Spencer, and I take ourselves away and self-choreograph 'Shake Your Groove Thing'. We just make it to the end of the song when Simon calls us back into the main room to put it together with Nicki Wendt's hilarious version of Bob's Asian wife's 'ping pong' scene.

Then we rehearse the scene in Alice Springs where Tick finally meets his son. He's played by Scott Irwin, and he's around six foot two. It's beyond ridiculous. Simon's decided to get a real boy in for the performance. We're all aghast. The show is peppered with highly adult material. We resolve to have the child ushered in and out of the performance at appropriate times, so he's not subjected to our filth.

The child arrives on Tuesday afternoon, and everyone fusses over him. He's a pro, having been in plenty of other shows. He already knows his lines. We block him into the scenes, and he turns out to be a real show stealer.

Tomorrow is the performance. To my utter disbelief we've got nearly the entire show blocked. It's utter chaos, but we've got there. Nerves begin to hit me. It may just be ninety minutes of something we've banged together, but to me it really matters that it comes off well. The anticipation is growing in all of us.

I look about. Actors carry pieces of script around, and gaze vaguely to the horizon as they try to cram another scene in. People hover around the piano trying to squeeze their head around a harmony or melody line. In my every spare moment, I find myself singing through 'Lullaby', like it's a mantra.

At the eleventh hour I'm given another song: 'Always On My Mind'. I don't know it well, and I try desperately to cram the words into my head.

Wednesday arrives. There are still a couple of scenes to straighten out, and some songs that haven't been choreographed at all. Everyone's on edge. It's a bit like an opening night. The guest list is slowly feeding into the group's consciousness. We know the English producers, Garry McQuinn and Liz Koops, will be here, as well as Stephen Elliot, infamous theatrical producer John Frost, and various publicists, designers, and marketing people. For some reason, of all the personnel coming, John Frost is the one I'm most keen to impress. I can't be sure why. Maybe it's because I feel I owe him.

We've worked together before when I played Cornelius Hackl in his production of *Hello, Dolly!* Back then he was getting ready to stage *Crazy For You*. I had my eye on Bobby, the lead role. I'd been told by everyone who'd seen it that it was a fabulous show, and a great role for me, but it required an actor who could tap dance. I was touring with *Hello, Dolly!* for months, so I decided to throw myself into tap lessons and see if I could crack the role. I don't know if Frosty heard about this or not, but he called me into his office and asked if I'd like to do the role. I said I'd love to, but I didn't know if I could dance it. To my utter dismay he offered to fly me to London to see the show and find out. It was such a generous nod to his confidence in me.

We had a break from *Hello, Dolly!* for a week between Brisbane and Perth, so I jumped on a plane to see the show and meet the choreographer, Susan Stroman. Half dead with jet lag, I went straight from the plane to the theatre. I plonked myself down to watch the show, and I can vividly remember my palms sweating in anticipation as the lights went down and the overture began. The curtain rose, and Bobby entered for his first number. Exactly twenty seconds in, I realised that the only way I could have possibly done this show was if I'd been dancing since I was a foetus. I felt sick. No amount of tap classes would get me up to scratch for this. Frosty had totally done his dough on me. Shit, shit, shit!

The next day I met Susan Stroman. Overnight I'd concocted a devious little plan to extract details from her of which number from the show she was going to use in the auditions. This strategy was not designed to actually get me the role, only to stop me being completely humiliated at the auditions. At my dancing level, it still took me hours to learn a few steps. If she tried to teach me *anything* from this show, I would look like a complete idiot. I knew I could get my hands on a tape of the routines from the show, so knowing which number would be used in the audition would allow me to get my teacher to learn the routine and then teach it to me beforehand. I wouldn't get the job, but at least I wouldn't make an arse of myself, or Frosty, for having had the insane confidence to suggest I could do the role.

I went to the theatre for the appointment with Susan. Her assistant greeted me with a distant handshake and instructed me to wait for Susan in an ornate, walnut panelled anteroom, adjacent to the theatre foyer. I felt like I was about to meet the Queen. I waited for a good five minutes in there. Then the assistant came back and announced that Susan was about to enter. It made me want to crack off a terrible fart before she came in, just to make things that bit more interesting.

Finally, Susan arrived. She thrust out a hand, and I greeted her warmly. I could tell by her manner that she intended to spend only a matter of seconds with me, so I had to drive the conversation towards the audition as quickly as possible. I needed the name of that routine. I cleverly asked when she expected to be coming out for the auditions and what they would entail. She ignored the question and asked me how long I'd been dancing. My plastered smile momentarily faded. 'Oh, years,' I answered. Then I popped the question: 'Which number will you audition with? I mean they're all so wonderful. Which do you intend using?'

'I Got Rhythm,' she said.

I knew it! I should have guessed! My plan was secured. I spent the rest of the fifteen seconds I had with her telling her what a *fabulous* time I was having performing a lead role in such an acclaimed show as *Hello, Dolly!* Then she shook my hand firmly and swept out of the room.

When I returned to Australia, Frosty wanted to know what I thought of the show and how I'd go with the dance. Lying through my teeth, I told him that it was a stretch, but nothing was impossible. The language was vague, but the mood was upbeat, and he seemed to be happy with that.

Through terrible subterfuge, I borrowed the videotape of the dance numbers for the show from the *Hello, Dolly!* company office. I was under strict instructions that they were for my eyes only, and I was to return it the moment I'd finished watching it. Of course, I went straight off and had it professionally copied, gave it to my dancing teacher, and started learning 'I've Got Rhythm'.

By the time the auditions came around, I knew the number and had been working on it relentlessly.

That morning, I prepared at length. I warmed up my voice, ran through the number several times, and invoked the support of my dead ancestors. I went to the theatre and waited onstage for the audition. Three of us from *Hello, Dolly!* were auditioning for Bobby, which we did as a group. Susan swept in cheerfully, without a whiff of the status she demanded in London, and greeted me without the slightest glimmer of recognition. This may have been a blessing in disguise. We lined up behind her, ready to start.

'Okay,' she commanded. 'We'll be learning 'Things Are Looking Up.' She proceeded to launch, very quickly, into a mass of incomprehensible tap steps. This was not the song she'd promised! No, no, no!

I was in too much shock to take in the first couple of bars, so I was already behind the eight ball. The others had got the gist early, so she continued on into the next few bars. They were both keeping up, and then there was me, loping around at the back of the group like a sad, unco Frankenstein monster. It soon became so excruciatingly embarrassing that I eased my way off the stage and out into the lonely, Western Australian sunshine. I cringed all the way back to my hotel, imagining the story Frosty would be told of my ghastly humiliation. I shook my fist at my ancestors at the ease by which they'd let me down.

I've never worked for Frosty since, and I can't be sure if it's because of this particular unfortunate incident. Regardless, I was determined not to look bad in front of him today, just in case.

Right up to the assembling of the audience, the cast is drilling routines, songs and dialogue. Actors—their faces set in panic—seek you out and speak rapidly at you, reminding you about some moment we rehearsed days ago, which you've apparently forgotten.

The audience files in. It's large, around thirty. I know many of them, and I receive warm waves from a range of people, some of whom I can't place. I stay away from them, choosing to hover at the back of the rehearsal room in order to keep my focus and not be distracted by who's there. But there's a carnival atmosphere, and some of the cast choose to 'work the room'. The nerves are palpable both from the cast and from the audience. There seems to be a lot riding on today.

Simon calls the room to order, and true to form makes a witty speech about how shambolic this is going to be, how far we've come in the few days we've had, and how terrified we all are. He explains that some of the songs and routines don't exist, in which case he may step in and explain what's going on. Some songs will be sung, and some will be mimed to a CD. I've placed my script to one side of the room, opened at the first place where I know I'm going to need help.

Simon takes his seat, and the show begins. It's like leaping into the breach. There is an overwhelming sense of anticipation from the audience, who already seem to be behind us. They laugh at jokes right from the beginning, excited and supportive. I feel my concentration as sharp as a pin. I look around the room, and everyone shares this steely focus. Amongst the nerves, there's a determination to ride this baby home. I'm guessing the reason we've been selected for this process is the depth of our experience and skills, and I can already see everyone unpacking their boxes of tricks. Everyone's performance has gone up several notches since rehearsal, and parts of the show, which were tentative and uncertain even yesterday, are being played with a brave confidence today. Tony Sheldon is a study in all that is wonderful about performers. To watch him you'd think he'd been doing this show all his life. He inhabits the drama and finds every laugh in the gags. He is, in every respect, 'on'. As I'm working, part of me watches in wonder at his brilliance. Watch and learn, I tell myself.

I know my job today is to tell Tick's story. As the showing continues, I focus all my attention on that. I try to use every scene to play how this man feels about the imminent meeting with his young son.

The time flies. Before we know it, we've done most of the first act, and I haven't forgotten a single line. If something is not on the tip of my tongue, I make it up. If

I become confused about where I'm exiting or what I have to do next, it's easy to signal my confusion to the audience and get a sympathetic laugh. The mood in the room is buoyant. The audience is right with us, laughing heartily along the way. They clearly like the characters and want to follow their journey.

At last we near the end. It feels like we've run a marathon, and the beer that will follow can't come soon enough. As we finish, the audience erupts in thunderous applause. We're all thrilled. We've truly pulled something out of the bag.

Afterwards, we mill around with the audience and drink beer. The feedback is astonishing. There's an overwhelming consensus that the show has real potential. I head outside for some air and bump into Stephan. He's effusive, and tells me how he now feels like this can work as a show. I can't believe my ears. My first impressions of him as being remote and grumpy are blasted away as I realise that his bad mood was fuelled by the fact that he had never believed this idea could work. Now he's a convert he comes across as witty and relaxed.

As much as Spud and Ross have been instrumental in getting this together, Simon has been the absolute saviour of the project. Of anyone, Simon has doggedly put in the hard yards, hammering away at the script till the early hours and then bringing in the pages the next day. He's conjured the show from the ashes of the first day, and made it a piece that seems strong enough for the producers to put their faith into.

I head home, full of stories for Annie and feeling genuinely thrilled with how it went. Part of me is dreaming that the show will get up, and somehow the producers will use me in the eventual production. However it plays out, I'm fascinated by what will happen next with this show, which seems to be taking on a life of its own. I feel that I've had real input in turning it into a reality. Tick, tick, tick. Now it's just a waiting game.

Chapter 3

Knock on Wood
The Auditions

Four months have evaporated since the workshop—and so has the promise of this year being a fabulous year for work. My diary is gradually becoming an optimistic but ultimately pointless waste of my January expenditure. We subsist on a steady diet of voice-overs and corporate gigs. Those heady days of early January, where work was piling in, seem far away indeed.

My film script was well received and even earned a live reading with some fine actors. It won't go into production anytime soon, but it's like having money stuck away in shares: there's the potential for something to happen with the script in the future, so I'm happy for it to be there in the background.

When work is light, rumours abound about *any* potential job. Actors leap on the whisper of a gig like a hungry pack of dogs. Nothing is bubbling up about *Priscilla* though. I've only had one phone call from Lisa that gave any hint of their intentions. The producers have asked for my availability from August onwards, stressing that this is in no way an offer. Lisa and I decide they're a bunch of teasers.

I've also heard a rumour that Simon is in London, having discussions about whether the show should actually go ahead or not, but this is unreliable, and there's no word of any decision having been made.

One night after a show, I'm chatting in the bar with the theatre manager of Her Majesty's, when he sympathetically confides that the finances haven't come together for *Priscilla*, and it's dead in the water. If it goes on at all, it won't be until 2007. My year immediately takes a further nosedive.

But finally in early May a buzz begins. Someone I know tells me they're auditioning for *Priscilla, Queen of the Desert*. It's like an alarm clock ringing. Wake up, sleepy head, the day has just begun. I immediately call Lisa. She addresses me in that tender tone she uses when the news is bad. 'It's not looking good, Jezza,' she says.

The word from Amanda Pelman (the casting director) is that they are after 'names' for the show, and that they're not really interested in seeing me. I scrape my guts off our polished floorboards, paid for by musical theatre, and curse reality television shows as the root of all evil for giving the entertainment industry its seething appetite for 'celebrity'.

Deep down I'd anticipated this, but it comes as a terrible combination punch to the guts. Wounded, I ask Lisa, through teeth trying desperately not to sound gritted, to remind Amanda that although it's been a few years since I've been in musical theatre, I'm not without a track record. Gently, she reassures me she will, but we both know Amanda's only looking after the best interests of the show.

I try to be philosophical, magnanimous, brave, but the reality is that knocks like these seem to come in clusters. Only weeks before, I'd auditioned for a job in a

Production Company show. It had constituted only about two weeks of work, but feeling the need to get out and actually do something I'd thought I'd have a bash. It had been nearly two years since I'd worked a full-time job, and I was getting toey. I knew the creative team for the show well, and had worked with them on a number of occasions. I thought they'd be thrilled to work with me again. My hope was that my track record with them would count for something, and they'd either just give me the job or say, 'Jeremy, this one's not for you,' sparing me the need to audition. But, no, I'd to endure a number of awkward auditions, waiting way too long in freezing corridors with humiliatingly talented kids straight out of drama school, until I was finally ushered in to strut my stuff, brimming with embarrassment and choked with hurt.

When Lisa rang to say I didn't get the job I totally crumbled—all for two lousy weeks of work.

This all sounds very dramatic, I know, and to be honest the life I share with Annie is a quiet, blessed existence. I bring home enough money to support our lifestyle, which consists of looking after our two little boys, eating well, paying the mortgage, and writing when I can. It can be scary as hell. At the beginning of most weeks we don't know how we're going to make what we need to survive, but as the week rolls on jobs come in and most of the time we make it. Some weeks we do really well, and other weeks we miss the mark. It can wear you down, but ultimately I'm a stay-at-home dad who has watched his sons grow up. It's a life of kinder fundraisers, football in the park, and space adventures in the playground. It's not a champagne lifestyle, but it's full of love. It's the reason why, for the last six years, I've resisted going for any work that would take me away on tour. For the ten years prior to that, Annie and I were constantly on the road with some show or other.

A week later, Lisa rings back to tell me that *Priscilla*

want me to audition after all. This is a happy conversation, but it's also excruciating to think that I'll be auditioning in front of the same creative team who has seen me perform the entire show already. Just to make sure I wasn't tricking them, they want to see me do a three minute scene from the show, as well as a couple of songs. I feel conflicted, but at least I have a foot in the door.

Days after this news, Annie and I see a friend's play at the MTC. As we drive out of the Arts Centre car park and pull up at the lights, I see Simon Phillips in the car next to us. It's an unbelievable coincidence. Simon physically jumps in the air as he notices us madly gesticulating at him from the car next to him.

He launches into bad car mime, imploring us to pull over. When we do, he leaps across his bonnet and says he's been trying to get my number to explain why I had to audition. Apologising profusely, he tells me that the producers want to compare me to the other people auditioning for the role.

God bless you, Simon. A flicker of warmth returns to my icy heart. I pick Simon's brain about what the producers have in mind. Do they intend to 'cast up' (populate the show with names), or are they going to let the show be the star? This is something he clearly can't predict. One of the producers is deadset on getting big names, but others want to make the show the star. A mass of inappropriate questions logjam in my throat. I have so many that the conversation soon grinds to a halt, not for want of material, but for my inability to sift quickly enough through which question to fire off without leaving me red faced later. We've danced around the issues enough to leave me in no doubt that he's keen to have me in the show. I'm so relieved. Perhaps I've worked my way through my nasty cluster of disappointments.

My audition is set for the morning of the 18th of May, at the Princess Theatre in Melbourne. They've asked me to prepare a disco song, and also learn a scene and the song 'Always On My Mind'.

The idea of singing a disco song sends me into a tailspin. Disco is the domain of the disco diva, and no self-respecting white male should dare to go there. I spend days trawling a sea of internet sheet music sites for an appropriate song. They all offer a taste of how the music sounds when played on the piano, and they invariably sound like Granny has fired up the Lowrey and is playing her best church version of 'Carwash' or 'Best Disco In Town'.

I try 'Knock on Wood' because Bowie sang it. I download it and bash through it a few times, finally settling on it as my offering. I secretly hope they'll spare me the indignity of actually having to sing it though.

I want to sing beautifully at my audition, so I attempt to breathe some life into my rusty vocal chords. I sing scales, trying to capture that liquid feeling when your voice is fit and seems to pour effortlessly out of you like syrup. I run the scene a few times, but I know it back to front and feel I'm just hammering the life out of it. I try to eke out any nuances that I may not have discovered previously, but instead I find myself daydreaming about who on the panel will want me, and who will be eager to kick me off the list.

Haunting scenarios of me forgetting lines or screwing up assault me. The bad devil voice on my shoulder is having a day out. There is, of course, an angel voice too, but that can be just as destructive. You have to temper your voices for an audition. Going in too confident can be a complete turn off. You might imagine that you have some extraordinary grasp of the character, which no other actor on the planet has. I once auditioned for the role of a mad scientist in an American film being shot in Australia. For some reason I thought making the character French was a brave and groundbreaking idea. The problem was I don't do a decent French accent, so in the audition I prowled around the room ranting madly with an unintelligibly thick accent from somewhere between Bombay and Bosnia. The casting director stopped me halfway through my first read, and with a look of sympathetic but horrified pity quietly asked me what I thought I was doing.

Before the audition I have two voice-overs. This is a useful diversion to break up my nerves, but I'm worried I might strike a difficult client who'll keep me longer than I've allowed for while they agonise over whether my read is 'too sexy for coffee'.

I've wrestled with what to wear. It can't be too casual—as I'll feel like I'm stating that *Priscilla* doesn't mean that much to me—but it can't be too dressy either, or I'll feel uncomfortably over groomed. I want to look handsome in case there's a spunk factor involved, and I also want to present an element of how the character would dress. I've chosen jeans, comfortable shoes, which I can move in, and a nice, slightly camp shirt. In spite of taking all this into consideration, I know that no one has ever got a role because of their choice of audition attire.

I can't be late, but I don't want to be too early either. I want to arrive right on time and sail into the audition without having to see or speak to anyone else auditioning.

My nerves accelerate as I cruise, looking for a car park near the Princess. I'm early, so I'm hoping I'll have to drive around looking for parking spot. Of course I find one almost immediately and directly out the front of the theatre, which makes me frustratingly early.

Before I feed the meter, I run the lines and the lyrics again. I invoke the support of my dead ancestors. I try to focus through the nerves. I see a parking officer approaching, so I feed the meter.

I head towards the Princess through a perfect Melbourne, autumn day. The oaks would be dropping their yellow leaves if there were a breath of wind. A day like today in this part of the city demands a Vivaldi underscore to accompany the soaring columns of

Parliament House, which dominates the top of Burke Street, the generous and welcoming opulence of the Hotel Windsor, and the jewel in the crown: the Princess Theatre, which sports an exacting and sumptuous restoration to its former glory as a Victorian treasure. Unlike so many Sydney theatres, she's avoided the developer's ball, dilapidation, or the ugly stick.

I tread unsteadily towards the foyer, reflecting that this is where I made my professional debut in the theatre at the age of eight. My uncle was company manger for the Australian Opera. They'd pick up small roles as they toured the country with their latest season, and he'd populate the juvenile roles with my brothers, my sister, and me. I had two lines in Italian in *Gianni Schicchi*, which made my parents proud. On opening night I got them the wrong way round. I hope that's not an omen for today.

I enter the marbled foyer dead on time, and search for an underling to tick me off a list. They say they're running behind. *Great.* This gives me just that little bit more time for my nerves to build to fever pitch, and for me to bump into the other auditionees. I don't want anything to destroy my focus or confidence. When I auditioned for *Sunset Boulevard* I was feeling pretty good, confident, focused, as I waited to go in. Then Hugh Jackman walked out, having just done his audition. The panel were all over him, and he looked like the movie star just waiting to happen that he was. He beamed at me, we embraced, and he wished me good luck. But the damage was done. I knew they'd already found their Joe, and it was all I could do to wobble in and go through the motions.

Across the foyer I glimpse an actor I know, and I'm spotted before I can escape. We greet warmly and try to appear calm. We giggle about having to sing a disco song. He tells me he couldn't think of one and asks what I've chosen. I hold up my sheet music to 'Knock on Wood', and he thinks I'm offering to lend it to him to sing—and gratefully accepts!

For the moment I'm not too worried. Why shouldn't he sing it? But then I remember he's a fabulous singer! What if I can't follow it? It's too late to turn back though as, clutching my music, he waltzes into the audition ahead of me.

I'm still reeling with the ramifications of this when suddenly Simon appears. He's come out specifically to see how I am. I say I'm nervous, but I'm truly heartened by his personal attention.

He tells me not to worry, as they haven't seen anyone they like yet. I'm staggered. This is such a positive admission. My mind floods with the doubtful possibility that maybe I don't actually *have* any competition. Except the guy who's got my fucking sheet music. I sheepishly 'fess up about my ridiculous offer to the previous contestant. Almost everything amuses Simon, but this one totally cracks him up. He wishes me luck, and he heads back into the theatre, still chuckling.

I try to conceal myself from anyone else who may be in the race as I run the lyrics of my song. I couldn't know it any better, but the devil voice keeps warning me I'm going to forget it. My guts churn. The minutes throb painfully as I wait endlessly for my execution.

Finally, the guy before me exits looking slightly downcast. He's probably already running through what's just happened, sifting the moments into 'not so good' and 'terrible'. I break his morbid daydream and ask for my music back. He tells me it's still inside, and he gives me an encouraging thumbs up.

My turn. I make a last ditch effort to focus, to remind myself I've done this a hundred times and this is what I *do*. The underling calls my name. There's no backing out now. She opens the heavy, draped doors to the theatre and gestures me inside.

One last deep breath and I step into the netherworld of the audition, where everything becomes about the sell. I'm now all about the next twenty minutes. Real Jeremy stops, and auditioning Jeremy begins. Auditioning Jeremy's not a real person; he's a product that is glinting on the supermarket shelf, tempting you to buy him.

Inside, the producers are building a corporation. But unlike most businesses, this one is put together like a Meccano set. This piece goes with that, and this one needs to do that for this bit to work. My next twenty minutes needs to be tailored towards being a bit they need.

I make my way past the empty, velvet seats to the side stage entrance. The theatre still smells like a theatre even in the daytime: lusty and opulent. The curtain is up, and I can see the long panel of creatives facing away from me towards the back of the stage. They're cracking jokes and laughing.

I'm led up the stairs from the auditorium to side stage. The readers stand like soldiers at ease waiting to be summoned to act with me. One of them is an old friend, and I give her a distracted squeeze on the way past. She beams frantically at me, then I walk out onto the stage.

The intimidating line-up of the entire production team turn as one and focus their attention on me from behind their laptops. I crack a funny about them secretly browsing porn. They laugh, and I make my way down the long table sharing out hugs and kisses by the dollop. The nerves have created a heightened 'me'. Everything I'm doing is just that bit over the top. I have my foot on the charming pedal, and I'm gunning it. While they continue to laugh, I continue to joke. My eyes flick nervously to Frosty. His body language is closed, and he's not laughing much. I suspect he doesn't want me. He wants to 'cast up'. I just know it. Amanda Pelman has already hugged and kissed me profusely though, so maybe things have changed with her.

Simon calls us to order and announces proudly, almost bitchily, that they didn't let the person before me sing my song. They all crack up, and I feel like I'm part of a tiny conspiracy. When the laughs die down it becomes clear that the business end of this shindig must now begin. Simon asks if I'd like to sing 'Always on My Mind' as part of the scene. I leap at the chance, as it's an opportunity to feed the song into the audition in a way that suits me best: an actor singing as part of a dramatic moment, rather than just getting up to sing.

Spud summons me to the piano to have a quick sing through the song. Like the underhanded sneak that I am, I use the bonhomie to try to negotiate the song down a key or two. Spud is onto me and cuts me off at the pass. In fact he goes further, asking to hear something rocky, tearaway. I don't *do* tearaway. And that's when I get a chill. It's not so much Frosty I've got to get around, but Spud. He wants a big voice for this role, and mine is a croony, gentle one.

I assure him that I've sung rock 'n' roll before in *Buddy* and in bands, and that I just need to get back into some form. I can see he's unconvinced. He wants to hear it for himself. I assure him I'll give 'Knock on Wood' a belt when I sing it later. I don't even convince myself with that statement.

We sing through 'Always on my Mind', and he's happy with where I'm pitching it. Now it's time to do the scene. I wander away from the panel to focus myself. Acting is very different to the singing component of an audition, so I need to change my headspace. Tick is softer and more vulnerable than I am, and I need to touch that before I begin.

The readers approach in a posse. Simon places us in the space away from the table to give them some room—some perspective. From where I'm now standing, I can see past the panel out to the gaping auditorium, and the empty rows of seats. Something clicks into place. I'm in a bloody theatre; I need to bloody well perform.

With a nod from Simon, we begin. In an audition, when your blood is up and you're nervous, it's crucial to keep a tight control of your performance. It's very easy to overcook it. The scene is an emotional one, and the temptation would be to turn on the waterworks. I'm determined not to go there, only to stop at the brink—a tricky level to play in this headspace.

The readers are top notch and instantly adapt to my interpretation of the character. While we run the scene, I'm acutely conscious of a myriad of things. I keep tabs on the panel, how they're reacting, who I feel is with me or against me. I process the choices the readers are making with the text, and notice whether they're listening to my interpretation of it. I'm even aware of feeling slightly awkward performing in front of my old friend, like there's a tiny part of her judging me. It's a juggling act of the mind because, in amongst all this external monitoring, I'm giving a performance that is tight and controlled. I make sure I drive the scene and don't allow the readers to outshine me. If they don't react to where I place myself, I sweep around them so they have no choice but to respond to me.

And then the scene is finished. The readers back away and leave me to sing the song. I launch into it as part of the drama of the scene. I know parts of it sound good, and the deep resonance of the beautiful old theatre gives it guts, but then there are the top notes. The first time I go round them I slightly choke on them. I imagine Spud flinching. I've got another chance in the second chorus, and I go for it. This time I improve, but I'm worried they've heard it sung better over the last few days.

I come to the end of the song and finish. Unlike a performance, there is no immediate response to rank yourself by. There's no clapping or cheering, just polite nods from the panel. You have to use your instincts to judge how you've done. I scan the faces along the table to hazard a guess, but they're unreadable.

Spud's now in the driver's seat. He struggles to his feet and calls on me to sing 'Knock On Wood'. It's my worst nightmare. Summoning the dregs of the charm I have left,

I appeal to him to only make me sing one verse and a chorus. I cite the fact that I'm not a black woman from the 70's, and so I'm at a terrible disadvantage. With the glimmer of a smile, Spud grants this one.

He hits the piano and plays the song in a key that demands I belt the crap out of it. I can't tell if the gravel I try to put into it comes off as legitimate, or if I sound like I'm straining my voice. I self-consciously try to 'sell it'. One advantage I have is that the theatre is helping me out. I can hear the resonance of my voice coming back to me from across the stalls. Let's hope the creatives can too.

I finish the song and flick a glance along the table to assess the mood, but the audition is already over, and they've shut up shop. I get nothing back from them at all. Having given them the best I could give, I snap out of it and quickly head back the way I came in, kissing and hugging my way along the table in reverse. This time I'm a little less self-assured, and I try to gauge *the shine* in each of them as I go. Ross and Simon are beaming and in turn they each clap me with an affectionate hug. I make a special effort to joke with Frosty, testing his mood, and he responds warmly. I see this as a minor victory.

I wave farewell devotedly, as if I'm going away on some exotic journey, never to return, and I leave the stage. The panel begin to swarm, and I know they'll be discussing *me*. I shudder at the thought, and stumble unsteadily down the stairs back to the auditorium, now exorcising the need to actually be anything but little old me. This last twenty minutes has taken at least two years off my life, and I'm exhausted. I smile thinly at the underling on the way past, thinking only of escape.

When I hit the crisp autumn sunshine outside, my tension falls away like the melting polar ice caps. As I stagger, punch-drunk towards my car, a swirl of post-mortem thoughts descends upon me, and I swish them away like pesky ghosts. I stop dead in my tracks and shake myself out. I'm going to ignore any negative thoughts that present themselves. I resolve to be happy with having just done my very best in there. I regain touch with the sane world, switch direction, and head for China Town and a reward: a delicious bowl of roast duck noodle soup. Doris Day has the best advice for me now: Whatever Will Be, Will Be. Time to uncurl from the crushing pressure of trying to stay in this little game.

*

I don't have to wait long for an outcome. Lisa calls later in the afternoon to say I must have done okay because they want to see me for a callback tomorrow—this time in drag. The crushing pressure returns, but this time it's unfamiliar territory. I've never done drag, and now it seems this job depends on me pulling it off. I'm sick with nerves and apprehension. If I was worried about what to wear to the last audition, what the hell do I pluck from the wardrobe for this one?

To my relief they offer to provide the outfit and a make-up artist. All I have to do is show up and be transformed into a woman. Just another day at the office.

I arrive at the theatre to a completely different atmosphere from yesterday. It feels weekend casual, like the formality has drifted away on a cloud. It's as if the hordes braying at the gates of the production have been repelled and only a lucky few have made it through to the inner sanctum.

I'm walked by the underling, now my new friend, through the draped doors and up onto the stage. There's a dance call in full flight as I arrive. The audition panel spot me and wave warmly. It makes me feel special somehow. Ross is taking the dance call, and it looks like the beginnings of a show. It's very exciting to watch. One of the dancers is a well-known TV actor, and I hardly recognise her because she's so proficient in her steps.

The underling takes me backstage to a groaning make-up desk. The make-up artist turns out to be Jo, a woman I've worked with before on kids' TV, and we instantly cack ourselves laughing at the thought of her making me up as a woman. She gets a wicked look in her eye as she begins, like she's just about to roll me in the mud.

Drag make-up is an incredibly slow process. First you have to wax the eyebrows (not off, just to cover them) and then apply a base that the new colours can go over. Jo works quickly, but this still takes a good hour. She sketches new eyebrows high on my forehead, and then fill colours into the gap between my eyes and on my now soaring brow. I'm shaded, highlighted, and colourised, and beginning to look very funny—like a comic book version of myself.

She outlines my lips with pencil before filling in the gaps with a lipstick that drips with gloss. My lips now look like a couple of skinned watermelons.

As a final touch, Jo applies glitter into my eye shading. She stands back and laughs like a drain. I can't decide whether to join in or feel insulted. I don't want to move a muscle in case this new face, which feels like it weighs a ton, falls off into my lap.

The creative team waits patiently on stage for me, resisting the temptation to sneak a look. Ross is the first to crack and rush in for a peek. As he steps backstage and catches a glimpse, his face lights up. It's impossible to tell if it's pure revulsion or desire. He screams and says, 'Oh, my God,' over and over, like he's just discovered Christ. Simon hears the reaction and can't help himself. He rushes in and is instantly doubled over. I feel like a circus clown, and I don't have a vocabulary to deflect this kind of attention. Do I yell, giggle, or play along in character? I campily shoo them away, shaking the back of my hand at them like I'm Jeanne Little.

I'm still de-wigged. There's a nest of them to choose from, and I settle on being a redhead. It goes with the green frock they've provided. I fit the wig and turn to the mirror. To my horror, I'm *the* most ugly woman I've ever set eyes on. I look like a distorted Angelica Huston, or worse, Cher. But I can also see touches of my sister in there as well, if my sister were ever to be hit with the ugly stick. My heart sinks. I'll never get this job now, I think to myself. I'm way too ugly.

Not to be defeated, I practice a few struts up and down the backstage area in heels. I'm determined to walk like a woman and swing my hips convincingly, but it's much harder than it looks. I've watched women's hips all my adult life, and for all of that perving, I can't for the life of me work out how the hell they do it.

I know the creative team is onstage waiting eagerly for my debut. I decide to make a splash on my entrance, so I strike a theatrical pose in the doorway and wait for them to notice me. For at least twenty seconds my arsey, pouty, slutty pose goes unnoticed. But then, one by one, like slow motion dominoes, they all turn and discover the unbelievable transition before them. Laughter builds until it raises the roof. It's a combination of pure hilarity and bewilderment.

I begin a long, slow seductive swagger towards them. They are crying with laughter, but I fix them with a burning, womanly gaze. This of course makes it even worse. I do everything I can to shut out the laughter bubbling up inside me. I have to hold on here.

Deep down I feel confronted, a little foolish, and very vulnerable. I arrive at the panel posing and pouting above my sense of unease. After a very long time, the laughter peters out, and they wipe their eyes and try to decide what to do with me. I flirt outrageously with them, which creates little pockets of laughter that flare up like spot fires.

Simon suggests I sing a song. I'm not prepared for this. I haven't warmed up. I know it's the best thing to do, but I'm still so totally out of my depth in this garb. I'm a three-year-old behind the wheel of a Mack Truck. After negotiating with Spud about what to sing, I perform 'In The Wee Small Hours Of The Morning', perhaps the most beautiful torch song of all. He plays the intro and I strike a pose, leaning dramatically into the piano. Suddenly, it's 3.00 am, and I'm a fallen woman choking on tears and whisky in a smoky club.

As I sing, I hook into a very strange feeling. All men 'camp it up' at some stage, but there's always a point at which there's a nudge and a wink and you drop it. It's an escape mechanism to get out of the joke. But for the first time, I can't drop it. My job here is to drive this character, this *woman*, right through the audition and the song, and not desert her by dropping her off along the wayside. I have to remain a woman. The desire to cut and run is immense. It reminds me of scuba diving. The first time you're submerged for longer than is natural for survival, the body instinctively wants to head for the surface. You're breathing through a regulator, so you're not in any danger, but there's still a panic reflex that makes you want to make a break for the air above you. I have that same urge now—swim for the surface and manhood.

I struggle with keeping in character, acutely aware of what an ugly woman I am and how everyone's astounded eyes are searching me. I marvel at how some women can strip in front of a crowd of slobbering men.

When the song finishes, Simon wraps it up saying, 'That's it for today.' But I can tell no one wants to let me go. They haven't finished examining the freak. I'm desperate to know if I've done enough, that I'm not too ugly to play this drag character, but the mood is too silly to get any indication. As long as I'm standing there in a dress, I feel beholden to perform. My feet ache in the stilettos, and I want to somehow close the session off with a towering joke. I blow kisses and head back to the dressing room. A bunch of boys auditioning for the ensemble are dragging up too. There's a scuffle over my wig, as it's far and away the best to be had.

I disrobe, de-wig, and get out of make-up. When I return to the stage it's late in the day, and the panel is now busy racing through the final auditions. In my boy clothes I'm no longer the star attraction. I bump into Michael Hamlyn, one of the producers of the film, and now a producer of the stage show. He seems like he's still recovering from my 'turn'. He giggles about how they took Hugo, Guy, and Terence out in drag as preparation for the movie, and confides in me that they fully intend to do this for me as well. I'm staggered. Has he just unwittingly blown the lid on where I stand in all this? An electric ball of excitement prickles inside my guts, and suddenly the enormity of this job hits me. I recognise just how much work it will be if I *do* get it. Learning the drag: the make-up on, the make-up off, walking in heels, embodying being a woman without suffering that piercing self-consciousness.

1. The ugliest woman I've ever seen. My first outing in drag.

For a different reason, I stagger out of the theatre again, possibilities whirring. I catch the train home a little dumb with shock, and imagine the research I'm going to need to do for this role. How would it feel getting on this train in drag? Would I have the courage to do it? Would people instantly recognise my masculinity beneath the make-up and girly fashion?

I look at the faces around me travelling home from work, and I smile to myself in wonder at how unusual my job is. An hour ago I was in full drag make-up and dressed as a woman singing a torch song. What did the guy next to me do? Sell mobile phones? I'm sure he wouldn't be travelling home so comfortably if I hadn't changed out of the dress. The world really is a pretty straight place. A true drag queen would have many stories to tell about that, I'm sure. I'm suddenly filled with admiration at their courage to be so different.

That night Annie and I go to the casino for the opening night of *Eurobeat*. This is a perfect way to take my mind off the audition and the terrible waiting game I'm now hooked into. Just as we're about to escape into the show, Tony Sheldon arrives. We're stunned to see each other. I tell him about my day in drag, and we piss ourselves laughing. I ask him how he went, and he sadly confesses he was told not to bother auditioning. He says they're looking for an international star for the role. I can tell by his face he thinks it's over for him. It's impossible to believe. Tony has everything the role needs. I can't fathom why they would bother looking any further.

The optimism I felt this afternoon now gutters. My guess is that if they don't cast Tony, they'll never cast me. The three leads will be big names. I try to make him feel better by reassuring him that I think there's no one in the country that could play the role better than him, but I can tell this is small consolation. We both drift off to watch the show only half concentrating, awash with scenarios of how this process will end up.

I hear nothing for five days. I wait until the following Wednesday before I call Lisa to find out what's going on.

I preface my call by reminding her how restrained I've been. She says she'll make a call and get back to me. It takes her until that evening to ring with the news of no decision.

That weekend I bump into Ross Coleman outside my house. We chit-chat for a while until I can't stand it any longer and probe him for whether I'm still in the game. He hedges diplomatically, but tells me I'm still in the loop. In a show like this, casting is done in departments. Each fights for their own needs. He wants dancers, Simon wants actors, Spud wants recording artists. He leans on this last statement, and I get his drift. *Spud.* My suspicion may be right. Spud might be my stumbling block. Ross wishes me good luck and trots off to slow roast a hare.

It's Wednesday again, and I'm doing a corporate gig. I'm performing to a bunch of bored executives to try and make their AGM bearable.

As we rehearse before the show, my mobile rings. I quickly bypass the call and continue rehearsal. But during a lull, I pick up the message. It's Lisa. My heart skips a beat. 'Jezza?' she says cheekily. 'Looks like you better get waxing. Call me.' Suddenly the earnestness of the corporate gig melts away. My life is once again about to profoundly change. Bewildered, I turn to the other actors in the group and announce my good fortune. Everyone celebrates, but I'm too stunned to really join in.

Dazed, I call Annie. I call my mum, who cries. I send out text messages. When I finish spreading the good news, I take a short moment for myself. I feel strangely upset. It's a profound sense of achievement and joy. I've been fortunate in my life, but *this* is like winning the lottery. I've been scooped up into the warm arms of musical theatre once more.

As my heart pounds, and I get my head around the new direction my life is about to take, I make a resolution to repay this good fortune.

Chapter 4
Can You Hear the Drums?

So I've made it into the citadel. This doesn't, however, get me any closer to the secrets of the inner sanctum. Information is being kept on a leash, and no one's talking about who else has been cast in the show. Dates for rehearsal and performances are not yet clear either. One piece of magnificent news is that Tony Sheldon has been cast as Bernadette. I'm almost as happy to hear this as I was to hear I'd been cast myself.

I'm called to Sydney for a photo shoot. The trip is run like a covert CIA operation. Nothing but threads of information are forthcoming. Beyond my flight time, an address, and instructions to bring three pairs of shoes, I know nothing. If I'm captured, there's no way I could squeal.

I'm gripped by a creeping fear that I'll have to get into drag for the photos, and I don't feel ready. It's a song I haven't learnt the tune to yet, and I don't want to sing it if I can't even hum it.

The cab locates a modest doorway down an impossibly thin Surry Hills laneway. I get my first whiff of the humid Sydney air as I stumble over uneven paving stones to the hidden studio entrance, hulking my bag of shoes.

The door is ajar, and I push politely through it. Inside, every surface is white, and the place smacks of the big time. There's a small gathering of people with an inner urban, professional cool. They nod to me—their version of friendly—and gesture for me to climb the white stairs beside me.

I pass framed headshots of former clients such as Elton John and Brett Whiteley, and I arrive at a state of the art photographic studio—also white. Through to the rear I can see movement inside a giant dressing room. Still operating under my own steam, I creep through the doorway and arrive at my first official engagement since getting this job. I find a man already half made up as a woman. My heart beats faster.

Another man rushes to greet me. It's Carl, the executive producer. He carries himself neatly and has a refined British manner. Dressed in a suit, he could be a businessman, if he wasn't betrayed by the slight whiff of wicked campness. He's my first official contact with the show, and it's quite exciting to shake his hand and have him welcome me into the fold.

He guides me over to meet Nick Hardcastle, the man who is half made up as a woman. Nick is already camping it up as he is worked over by the traffic-stopping Cassie, the make-up designer for our show and for the original film. Nick's clearly loving the experience, and it's impossible to believe this queen is actually straight.

Carl announces the actor who's been cast to play Felicia. Spencer McLaren hasn't been as lucky as Tony and me. The producers have gone for Daniel Scott. He's still performing in *The Dusty Springfield Story* in Perth and wasn't available for the photo shoot today. Nick is his understudy and has generously offered to take his place.

Nick beams mutely at us in the mirror, clearly at the ready to cause untold carnage when he's unleashed.

The question I really want answered is whether I'm going to be next in that make-up chair, and as if he's read my mind, Carl reassures me that I won't have to frock up today. I instantly relax. He says a stylist is coming in with some outfits, and we'll be doing some 'civvies' shots with Tony Sheldon, Nick, and me.

Fernando, the stylist—of course his name is Fernando. Can you hear the drums?—will be in soon with a variety of outfits for me to try on and be photographed in.

Lizzy Gardiner and Tim Chappel rush in with the outfit Nick will be wearing. These are the Academy Award-winning costume designers of the film, who will also be designing the show. I'm ridiculously shy with them, and since we haven't been officially introduced, I hang back and just grin mutely. They fuss over the last, minute details of the outfit, which is a work of genius. It's a pink dress, adorned with a highway—complete with road kill—which runs from bottom to top, and capped off with a plastic wig, which sports a large headpiece in the shape of Uluru. Priscilla is spelt out with gold letters, which are spiked into rock like fence posts. It's fashion's version of a really clever stand-up routine.

Tony Sheldon sweeps in. He makes a beeline for me, throws his arms around me, and beams. For a moment we laugh and hug warmly. 'I'm so glad it's you,' he coos, and I say it straight back at him.

Conscious he's left a trail of eager greetings in his wake, he turns and doles out generous hellos to everyone. But I'm the main game now, and we're both desperate to catch up on any gossip, so he quickly returns his attention to me. We haven't spoken since the night at *Eurobeat*, and there is much to say.

Tony is a theatrical switchboard. All gathered theatre intelligence flows through him. There's nothing he doesn't know. He says how happy he is that I got the role and then adds gravely that there are a lot of people out there who wanted it. He tells me there was a list of theatre luminaries who all called him one by one as they learned it wasn't going to be them playing Tick.

Tony was only offered the role in the last few days and is still awash with relief, delight and exhilaration. He was convinced he'd lost the role to a big overseas star and had been despairing about it. He'd heard talk that a list of 'names' had been approached, but were either too expensive or had declined.

He tells me that Daniel Scott was only offered his role yesterday. We draw closer and conspiratorially speculate about which members of the production team were *for us* and which were *against us*. When did they throw out their agendas and cast from their hearts?

Carl observes our hushed gossip session and comments on its intensity. We chuckle and turn away. I realise Carl is in possession of all the facts to which we've been speculating, and I now know beyond anything that in the not too distant future I'll be getting him very drunk and unlocking these secrets.

Once our chit-chat runs out of puff, I decide to get some news from the horse's mouth, and I ask Carl who else is in this little concert of ours. He tells me that John Wood is out of the picture for Bob. Billy Brown is playing him. Genevieve Lemon is playing Shirl, and Marney McQueen is playing Marion, my wife. I'm surprised. I thought they'd have cast someone from television for this role. I comment that I don't know her, and with a defeated shrug Carl says, 'Simon. He likes to work with actors, not stars.' He quickly corrects himself and says, 'Of course that's not the case with you, Jeremy. You're a star.' I smile at his polite British sense of loyalty.

A shortish man staggers in, concealed under a stack of suit bags and shirts. The only hint there's a person under there is the legs sticking out. This is Fernando, a sweet looking man who could dress you by reading your horoscope. Tony and I sift through his offerings to find something that most represents our characters in the show. I find a nice shirt and try it on. Tony says, 'Hey, that's mine!'

'Sorry, have you already chosen that?' I reply.

'No, it's my *actual* shirt.'

Nick is already in the studio getting snapped. He's an absolute natural in drag. I draw courage from him, a straight guy who is letting the outfit take him over. He pouts and snarls and teases his way through his session.

Then it's my turn. I step into the blazing lights. For the next few minutes I'm 'on'. I can't hide behind the drag like Nick's just done, but I need to be effervescent for the lens or we'll be here all day trying to get the shot. As the camera snaps, I pose my guts out and think of England. I give the confident look, the delighted look, the outrageous look, the sexy burn, and everyone's favourite, the wacky look.

Tony steps up to the plate. He mocks a coronary as the first blinding flash hits him. Everyone laughs. It's his way to break his own ice. His session is superb. He seems so at home and unselfconscious.

New technology means you can look back at the shots immediately on a large computer screen. It's fantastic, no guessing. If it's worked you can shut the gate and go home.

We get the shots we need in around twenty-five minutes, and the day is over. Everyone vanishes so fast I'm not sure I haven't missed some whispered instruction to meet somewhere else. But our work here is done, and I soon find myself fleeing from all the white, back out into the balmy Sydney day.

I meet a friend for lunch. She's up from Melbourne for the day and is brimming with gossip about the show too. Not only does she know a few others who missed out on my role, she also knows who the casting agent's favourite was, and it wasn't me. It's all chat, and maybe some of it might be true, but it gives me the strangest feeling of being in the middle of something. I'm on the ride, but I don't quite feel the wind in my hair yet.

My meal arrives and the aloof waiter places it before me. I'd asked him directly if the bulb artichokes with flat pasta and French goat's cheese was hearty. He'd said it was. What he places before me is a bird-sized insult of a meal. I should have ordered the steak. I look around the bistro and realise the menu has done its job of luring a clientele of well-dressed professional women in their forties. I see a slim, attractive woman picking at a tiny salad, and I think to myself that I'd better stick with the artichokes if I want to fit into a frock.

Chapter 5
Blast Off
Press Launch. 20th June

Everything goes right for my trip to Sydney for the launch of the show. My first call tomorrow morning will be at 7.00 am on Channel Seven's *Sunrise*, so for the sake of an earlier night I try to weasel my way onto the 7.00 pm flight, rather than the previously booked 8.00 pm flight.

Judging by the sour demeanour of the check-in girl it's never going to happen, but she stuns me, and without a word, or looking up from her computer keys she hands me a fresh boarding pass. A human being *is* lurking in there somewhere. When I arrive at the hotel, The Star Casino, I'm upgraded because they don't have any non-smoking rooms in my class. I'm liking the trip so far.

This is the first publicity junket I've done for over ten years. I used to be a pro. When I did musical theatre I used to think nothing of flying across the country, staying at swish hotels, and spending the day talking to journalists about the faaaabulous show I was in. Usually it was followed by a ripe old booze-up with the producers. Now, all these years later, I'm eyeing the free body scrub in the bathroom and pinching the soaps for the kids.

I relish the peaceful solitude of watching TV in bed and eventually, almost reluctantly, flick off the light when the lids get heavy.

I wake at six with more than a few butterflies about what's in store for me today. How gracefully will I get back on the horse? I have a running sheet of how the day will unfold, and it's massive. Loads of interviews and lashings of meet and greets. I'm totally up to the challenge and am quite chuffed to be back in the limelight again.

While fun, these junkets can be demanding and unexpected. You have to be on your toes or else you can become flippant and end up coming across as a right prat to the journo you're talking to—and they love to punish you if you pull that one. A lot of actors cherry-pick what they will and won't do from these lists. It's prudent, but I've always been a slut and done everything I've been asked to do. It backfired once when I was in *Buddy*. On a massive publicity day in New Zealand, I didn't bother checking out what kind of show I was on for my first television appearance of the day. It turned out to be a kid's show, and I ended up singing a duet of 'That'll Be the Day' with a glove puppet, while dressed in a full Buddy Holly tux. The publicist stood away to the back of the studio trying to hide from me, but even as we went live to air nationally she couldn't escape me glaring furiously at her across the studio throughout the whole song.

I chow down on some fruit salad, which is all my queasy stomach can handle after the dog food I ate on the flight last night. I shower, groom, check nasal hair, put on a suit and tie, swish my hair, and reach TV guest perfection precisely at the desired departure time.

Sunrise is terribly casual. You can see right into the studio from the street. As I wander around Pitt Street searching for the entrance, I suddenly become aware that maybe I'm actually on air, wandering around aimlessly in the back of the shot somewhere. Trying not to look lost (for the camera), I bump into Carl, who points out the Priscilla bus. It's a huge, silver vehicle lavished with feather boas, and sporting a giant stiletto with a long piece of silver fabric cascading behind it, which reflects the famous scene from the film. They're just about to do a drive by as a teaser for our spot, and the cameras are set up and ready to go. Carl's assistant, Clare, escorts me around the other side of the building to the entrance and steers me to the coffee machine. Tony arrives with Judith Johnson, our publicist. She's alight with energy and enthusiasm. All smiles, she introduces herself to me, which is her professional duty in case I haven't recognised her. It's ridiculous really though, as she's far more famous than me. We all head to make-up together.

After a flick of powder, we're ushered outside to wait for our spot. It's cold in the mid-winter early morning breeze. It doesn't even feel like the sun's properly up. Crowds gather. Something is clearly going to happen. We're joined by three drag queens, and I pity them their outfits because it's so cold. They've definitely drawn the short straw. Aside from having to endure the temperature, they've been here since 5.00 am getting into full drag make-up. One of them is Nick Hardcastle, and the other two are Damien and Trevor, the 'real' drag queens who have been cast in the show. They look amazing as they unleash themselves on an unsuspecting rush hour public. The only other time these girls would have seen this hour would be coming out of a dubious club somewhere. They are, however, lighting up the overcast morning and pulling an enormous crowd of bewildered office workers. They seem to be able to squawk flirtatiously in every direction simultaneously, in voices that can be heard from space.

As well as the drag queens, a gaggle of producers and creatives have gathered, all wearing feather boas. It's very gala. TV people arrive and wrangle us all in front of the bus. Tim and Lizzy are here for the interview, and with the shadow of their Oscar ever present they give the event immediate credibility. The producers cast a watchful eye over us as cameras arrive. The Sunrise hosts, Mel and Kochie, stride towards us. After an hour of waiting around, time speeds up. As the lens of morning TV turns to us, we become critical. Mel and Kochie shake our hands as the camera guy places us. The drags aren't speaking, so they don't have mics on. Thank God. Amidst the scramble to get the shot, the cheerful but impersonal chit-chat from Mel and Kochie, and the Queens jostling for front position, a tech calls out loudly and everyone goes quiet. 'In five, four, three, two...' he points to Mel.

The only sound now is the traffic and Mel's seamless introduction.

I'm standing next to her, out of shot. Trying to appear calm, I wink at Tony. I feel a bit like a deer in the headlights and hope it doesn't show.

Mel throws a question to Tony, and he picks up the ball like a pro. He sells the show in easy sound bites, giving dates of the opening night and talking up how wonderful it will be. Then Mel asks me how I am in heels. I quip that that's the only reason they gave me the job, then quickly divert to talking about the show. It feels a little clunky, but it's all a part of getting back on the horse. This stuff only looks convincing when you're accustomed to it. Kochie asks Lizzy about the costumes. She's terrific at this, as you just know she would be. The drags standing behind her shamelessly try to upstage her. She catches onto this and checks she doesn't have a knife in her back. 'Never turn your back on a drag queen,' she says.

Then it's over. The lens turns away from us once more and people scatter. Mel and Kochie are marshalled back inside. Producers evaporate. The boa-clad crowd disappears into the Sydney rush hour. I feel like the only one who hasn't been told there's a fire. I'm not sure who to follow. Suddenly alone, I take out my schedule and see

I have an hour or so off. My disorientation is broken as a cab charge is thrust into my hands, and I find myself speeding back to my hotel. Did that all just happen? My phone beeps as text messages come through from all those who've just seen my musical theatre career officially re-launched live on national television.

Before I know it, 11.30 am rolls around, and I head to the Sydney Lyric Theatre stage door, where the confirmed members of the cast will be gathering. We'll be presented en masse to an awaiting throng of media, for the official press launch. I feel like a curiosity amongst this young cast. They weren't even at drama school yet when I was doing musical theatre. They must question why *this guy* has been given the dream role of Tick. I'm relieved to see Danielle Barnes who—although still looking like a teenager—is a fellow veteran and someone I've worked with many times before. She gives me a wry grin as we privately celebrate still being around.

Lena Cruz is swinging off the handrail leading to the stage door. As if I'm an old friend she barrels up to me grinning cheekily and shakes my hand. She's Filipino, and she laughs hard as she says I don't need to guess who she's playing. She's, of course, playing Bob's ping-pong ball popping wife.

Smoking, and standing away from the group is Daniel Scott, the boy plucked from the ensemble of *Dusty* to play the Guy Pearce role of Adam/Felicia. I can instantly see why he's here. He's got star written all over him. He looks like a young Marcus Graham, and has an easy charm about him. I approach and introduce myself. He's confident and direct, but betrays a sensitive shyness. He laughs easily, as though the nerves have got the better of him today. I can see him slipping effortlessly into being the rock star of the show, the one they'll squeal for. I'm relieved to find him instantly likable, since we have such a long journey to travel together.

We head up in the lift to dump our bags, and I bump

into Simon. It's the first time I've seen him since the auditions, and I clamp him in a long, grateful embrace. The euphoria of the day seems to have caught even him off guard, and he looks nervous and edgy about the mountain we have to climb before October.

Outside is the huge silver bus I saw at Channel Seven. Carl wrangles us aboard, with strict instructions as to which order we'll be getting off. Our short trip will take us around to the other side of the casino, where the press has assembled. We're garnished with pink feather boas, which wilt and stain our clothes. The heat is sweltering inside the bus, and we all misbehave like school kids on an excursion.

The bus cranks its way up the hill towards the press call. They certainly didn't blow the budget on this old girl, and I'm slightly worried we won't actually make the distance. As we arrive, Frosty is in mid pitch. The size of the crowd takes my breath away. There's got to be a hundred people here. There's a collective gasp and applause as the bus lumbers towards them. We stop and remain on board, waiting to be introduced.

Simon's first out, and he leaps off the bus like a game show host to make an uncharacteristically tense speech. He introduces the Academy Award winners, Tim and Lizzy. They step out to generous applause. Then it's Tony's turn. Again a roar. I start to sweat as my name is about to be announced. God, I hope there's not a deathly silence. I step down from the bus, making sure I don't trip over. I stand for a moment as the crowd applauds me.

Once the cast have been introduced, Tony, Daniel, and I are given bottles of champagne to christen the bus with. This clearly hasn't been thought through properly. The press surge forward to within inches of us, and I realise that I'm going first. I hold the bottle like a baseball bat and make a couple of comical practice swings—then I make contact. There's a hideous metallic 'dong' as I connect with the bumper bar, but no breakage. Like a

Buddhist call to prayer, the 'dong' has awoken me to the reality that without a shadow of a doubt that when this bottle breaks, it's going to shower all those around it with speeding fragments of broken glass. It's going to be ugly. I take a deep gulp. Will this be the story of the press call? *Photographers blinded by shattered glass!*

Not having any options with the eager press poised for a photo opportunity, I squeeze my eyes shut and swing the bottle really, really hard. This time it explodes exactly as prophesied. Glass sprays outwards. There's a gasp from the crowd, my pristine suit pants cop a spray of champagne, and God knows where the rest of the deluge ends up. I look sheepishly at the crowd, and shrug off the embarrassment of having just doused myself with booze. I turn to Tony and grimace. At least he now knows what he's in for. It takes him three swings to break his bottle, with similar consequences. Daniel's turn. This is a boy who watches and learns. Avoiding the humiliation Tony and I endured, he makes his swing hard, and his bottle shatters the first time.

We gather in front of the bus, and with the drags behind us we pose campily for the cameras. It's then I notice my hand is covered in blood. There's so much that I can't tell where the cut is. I show Tony, who looks down in horror to his own hand to see that he's also dripping blood. We show Daniel. He opens his hand to reveal he's also bleeding. We all laugh, completely bewildered. How could this happen? It suddenly becomes *the* story amongst the press. Cameras click madly. Photographers want shots of the three of us nursing our bleeding hands.

Clare rushes up with tissues. I look over to Daniel and see him posing for a photo, looking down at his bleeding hand in mock horror.

Tony, Daniel and I are grabbed for a quick TV interview, and I make a special effort to be better than I was this morning. By the time we finish, the press has thinned.

The producers invite us to lunch. I deviously drill them for information about the auditions and cast, but they remain infuriatingly professional and tight lipped. The only gossip I get is that we've already sold three hundred tickets, unheard of before the official release.

After lunch, I'm to be measured for costumes, shoes, and wigs. An army of tailors, seamstresses, and wig people are at the ready, and every inch of my anatomy is measured. Even the corn on my foot is factored into the calculations for my high heels.

When I'm measured for my wig, someone covers my head in plastic wrap and then binds it tightly with packaging tape, until my whole head is a strange glossy ball. I look like the Pine Gap intelligence facility. They draw hieroglyphics onto it, and then ease the tape helmet off. I'm finally dismissed.

Next up is a Party Bookers' shmooze. This is crucial for kicking off ticket sales. All the influential group bookers are invited and plied with booze and finger food, as we pitch the show to them. Some of these bookers' launches can be enormous, up to five hundred people, but our producers have gone small and influential with this lot.

The first group is a bunch from the travel industry. Garry has drawn the short straw and does the introduction speech, something he's clearly not comfortable with. The content is on the money, but he speaks softly and nervously. He introduces Simon. I sense the producers haven't seen a Simon Phillips speech before. They need to strap themselves in. His speeches are infamous. He hits the stage with almost drunken enthusiasm, thanking Garry, saying that he's sure it was a fabulous speech but nobody could hear a fucking word of it. The crowd laughs and the producers shuffle nervously. Then he turns his attention to Lizzy and Tim.

'Oh, look over here,' he quips. 'We've got Tim Chappel and Lizzy Gardiner, both looking incredibly, self-consciously dressed down for the occasion. Ladies and gentlemen, these two have won an Oscar for their incredible costume designs for this show, but they've come dressed as street people. *We've* all bothered dressing up, why couldn't they?'

Tim and Lizzy's embarrassment becomes the crowd's delight. They all cack themselves laughing.

'And here's John Frost, another of our producers, with an amazing track record, including a Tony Award for *The King and I*. Ladies and gentlemen, he's kindly agreed to play a koala in the show.' (Frosty has a large, cuddly physique.)

The banter climaxes with him saying, 'The cast and crew have committed to giving their all to the show, now it's *your* turn to go away and sell some fucking tickets!'

The producers' anxiety peaks—but with little reason. Simon has the audience eating out of his hand. When the speeches are finished we all mingle with the crowd, selling them a show that doesn't exist yet. We tell them how fabulous it will be. They buy into the white lie and seem convinced the show will be a hit.

After telling our quota of fibs, we're ushered off to 'the Party Bookers' launch. This is less corporate and much more homey. There's a sea of grey hair at this one, and to their utter delight Simon is at his bawdy best. He tells them that if they miss seeing Tony and me in dresses they'll be missing out on the sexual thrill of a lifetime. They fall about laughing.

He introduces Tony, and they cheer like the Beatles have hit the stage. Tony makes a slick, witty speech, and they gaze adoringly at him. Then it's my turn. After two quickly slurped glasses of red wine my blood's up, and I fire off a few gags, which hit their mark. Daniel joins us. He's a natural, charming them instantly.

Simon finishes the speeches off by saying, 'If you like the young men standing in front of you then you'd better get booking, as they'll be straight back to the dole queue if you don't.'

I remind them I have two young sons to support, and without missing a beat, Daniel says he has two cats. The room is now a mass of old people on fire. We begin to mingle. Everyone I meet remembers me from *Buddy* and tells me how much they loved it. Tony is besieged by elderly women desperately in love with him. One snuggles up and says, 'Oh, Tony, if things were different...'

The schmoozing is spirited and genuine. It's not hard to sell a show that people already want to see, and this is a crowd who seem to have followed my entire career.

Carl leans into my ear and privately gives me the word: time to go. There's a cab downstairs waiting to take us to the airport. As we navigate our way through the adoring crowd, Tony is bailed up by an elderly man.

'Is Bluey Lamont your uncle?' the man asks.

Not wanting to hurt the old bloke's feelings, Tony lies and says, 'Yes.'

Tony has, of course, never heard of Bluey Lamont.

Suddenly emotional, the bloke grabs Tony's arm. Tony can't go anywhere now.

'Oh, we were in the army together. He was a wonderful man.'

Tony nods sympathetically.

'How *is* old Bluey? Is he still alive?'

Only half thinking it through, Tony says, 'No.'

The old bloke gasps, horrified.

'Oh, no!' he says, 'That's just *terrible*. He was younger than *me!*'

Chapter 6
Work Begins
Second Workshop. 21st – 24th June

I'm still processing yesterday's launch as I arrive at the MTC studios to workshop the new script. A bunch of the cast will assemble to put it through its paces. Now that I'm part of the project for real, I'm dying to see where it's at. Obviously, there have been endless script meetings and redrafts, arguments, tantrums, and budget restrictions—haven't there?

Over four months have passed since we made the offering of the last script. Plenty of time, one would think, to confirm what was good in the last one and what was needed to improve it. Drawings of costumes and sets will have been made, and ideas for the staging of dance numbers and set pieces must surely have been on the table by now. But, as usual, intelligence is scant. The executives of the citadel are tight lipped.

I arrive before anyone else and wait for the small gang of cast members who will be part of this workshop to assemble. Nick and Lena arrive, and we chuckle about the hijinx of yesterday. Nick can only shake his head in bewilderment when I tell him what a natural he is in drag. But where's Marney, the woman playing my wife? Who is this girl who beat off such fierce competition for the role?

Amelia Cormack fronts up, looking like someone who's just arrived home to their own surprise party. She's a young WAAPA graduate, who was only cast yesterday. She's had a dizzying twenty-four hours. She's flown down from Sydney to be part of the workshop. Her eyes project a sharp, inspired optimism. She giggles nervously as she asks if any of us know what we're going to be doing.

Finally, Marney sweeps into the room beaming at all and sundry. She rushes over to me, and Clare introduces us. I can tell that she's as keen to meet me as I am to meet her. I call her wife, and we fall into peels of laughter over nothing. This, it seems, is Marney's way. She has a charm about her that is like the tractor beam from an alien spacecraft. When it shines on you it instantly paralyses you, and then you are levitated into the air and drawn slowly, helplessly and inescapably into her hemisphere of beaming light.

We fire up the gossip and swap any information we have. Of course we're starved, so any tit-bits are worth repeating. I show her my champagne bottle war wound from yesterday, and we giggle over how surreal it all was.

Tony arrives, and the tempo goes up another notch. He and I huddle and speculate on what we're in for, and how the script will read. He's bursting at the seams. We're rounded up and taken into the rehearsal room. My eyes dart around the table for a pile of scripts, but the table is bare.

Simon welcomes us and explains the absence of scripts by saying Allan Scott can't make it in until this afternoon, so we'll wait for him to arrive before we read it. Until then we'll be working on music with Spud.

Spud takes over and assembles us around the piano. His brow is heavy, and I can see he wants to waste no time getting stuck into this. Our task is to fit some of the production numbers around the dialogue.

We begin with 'Go West'. This number sees the drag queens agreeing to travel to Alice Springs, brings the bus on stage, shows them packing the bus and then leaving Sydney. Spud needs to know exactly what action is involved in the scene, and how many bars of music are needed to work the song around the dialogue. Once that's bedded down he can begin to arrange the orchestra parts.

The scene begins with Felicia's speech, and she explains why she wants to go on the trip in the first place: 'To go where no queen has gone before, and conquer the outback in full Gautier, heels and tiara.'

The song begins as an underscore for the speech. In the absence of Daniel, Nick is playing Felicia in the workshop. He runs the lines a number of times as Spud plays the underscore to make sure it fits. When he's happy we move to the beginning of the song. We sing through to the first music break, which is where the bus appears. Simon imagines the time the bus will take to come on as the music plays out. The whole piece already seems to be in his head. Then the three Swedish backpackers, Lars, Lars and Lars hand the keys to Felicia, and there's dialogue to fit into the music. Spud switches a few bars around and negotiates with Simon where he wants things to go. Spud scribbles madly on his manuscript.

As the session goes on, I become a little self-conscious. Marney, Nick, Lena, and Amelia are fabulous singers. I'm working hard to keep up, but they're in another league. I begin to get a few tremors.

Spud stabs at the last lines of his arrangement with his pencil and seems satisfied. We go back to the start of the song and sing straight through it with dialogue. Simon looks like a crazed magician as he waves his hands around at his invisible bus, as he imagines its journey across the stage. When we reach the end, Spud and Simon are happy, and the song is chalked down as done. Spud leaps onto his computer and begins committing it to history.

Simon approaches me and says that we couldn't get the rights to 'Lullaby', the Billy Joel song that seemed to go so well at the first workshop. Instead, we'll be using 'Say A Little Prayer'. I get a few more tremors. This is a really tough song to sing. Didn't Aretha Franklin sing it? Just as I'm stewing about how it's going to sound, particularly in front of these incredible voices, Spud thrusts some music at me and suggests we have a sing through.

Now I'm nervous. I'm still a way off getting my voice back in shape, and my confidence is really low. Spud tries a key, and I ask for it to come down. He relents, but not as far as I'd like. We sing through it with the girls joining in at the second verse. I feel myself blushing. I want to stop and say, 'Look, I *will* get this together you know. It won't sound like this in two months' time.'

I head to lunch feeling a little downhearted. I can't tell if it's just me feeling like the pressure is on again after all this time in the music theatre wilderness, or if I'm instinctively picking up an element of resentment from Spud. I'm desperate not to be a paranoid actor, but I can't shake this feeling. My mood is flat, and the excitement I felt this morning has guttered.

Finally, the afternoon arrives, and we get to read through the script. Everyone's salivating. Allan Scott has joined us and placed himself like chief magistrate at the head of the table. There's no sign of Stephan, but he's sent Phil Scott in his place to be a kind of joke doctor and script editor. He presents like a character in a Woody Allen film, eyes alert, darting around the group, watching for secret code. He fires off jokes at a hundred rounds a minute, and still comes off with an enormous sense of credibility. I know his face from a thousand unplaceable performances.

The read begins. Now I'm on solid ground. Tick feels effortless as the pages turn. There have been some obvious changes since the workshop, mostly driving the script into coarser terrain. I can't believe how crude some of it has become. Lena laughs hysterically the ruder it gets, gasping for air and chanting, 'I can't fucking *believe* it.' But the script feels clunky. It's lost a lot of the gold that we'd found last time, and some of the really touching scenes have vanished completely.

As we finish I can see that Tony is disappointed. He looks across at me and privately shakes his head with disapproval. Simon remains neutral, waiting for comments, and it doesn't take long for the floodgates to open. Tony and I begin with our list of disappointments. Allan shares our opinion that it's clunky and too crude. Tony wants a scene put back where Bernadette fights with Adam for calling him Ralph in front of Bob, and I voice my concern that Tick has had all his jokes taken off him.

Allan and Phil vow to look at the script overnight, and we're released for the day. I leave feeling completely different about the whole process since last time. Then we had so much pressure on us to get the piece up and running. We had a deadline and a looming performance. This time, although we'll read the piece for the producers on Saturday, it's about connecting the dots and smoothing the way for rehearsals. Now I'm cast in the role there's no sense of 'What if?' about it. It's an intellectual rather than a theatrical process. Besides, now we have the luxury of having two writers in the room who can race away and work on any alterations we need. It's a little like shifting the furniture around the new lounge room and seeing what looks nice beside the china cabinet.

Thursday is much of the same: more testing music with dialogue, reading rewritten scenes, and *lots* of talk. The creases in Spud's brow deepen as the day goes on and as the reality of how much work he faces hits him. Personnel come and go according to their availability. Marney is performing in a play at The Arts Centre and so has to keep trotting off for technical rehearsals. Simon has his own MTC commitments too. His assistant tells me she has his every minute of every day planned and accounted for until the year 2010.

Friday. Ross Coleman arrives with a bunch of dancers, some of whom have been cast in the show, and some who have been hired for the morning. We're going to test 'Downtown' as the potential opener to the show. Spud has an arrangement ready, and Ross will stage it.

We gather around the piano, and Spud teaches the parts. I tentatively join in, but I can see I'm not going to be singing this one. Spud's arrangement already sounds like an opening number to a musical. Gone is the aspirational sentiment in the song, replaced with a kind of dirty R&B shuffle. It rocks along, and it's easy to get swept up in the power of it. The voices are strong and stabbing. I look across to Ross and see his brain whirling with ideas. Once the arrangement is learned, Ross launches himself at the routine.

As I suspected, I sit out of it to start with as the routine begins to paint a picture of Sydney streets at night. It's a harsh and alienating world, which Tick will eventually enter into. I watch in amazement as the choreography materialises from thin air. All kinds of scenarios spring out of the dance: robberies, lovers, junkies, mad people—all swirling around the stage while Amelia belts out the first verse. Voices join her as the song builds.

Finally, Tick enters through the chaos and walks towards the club where he'll perform 'Never Been To Me'. A dressing table mirror will come on with the stage revolve, and I'll get ready to go on stage to do my routine.

The whole number takes till lunchtime to choreograph, and it's a winner. The arrangement sounds fantastic, and the choreography is inspired. There's a palpable sense that this will work a treat. We perform it one more time, and it's videoed for future reference. We finish, and the cast instantly applauds Ross, who cowers from the adulation. He immediately talks it down, saying, 'No, no. I know what I'm going to do with it now.'

The afternoon takes us back to the script and the songs. Phil and Allan arrive with new pages to try out. They're like excited kids with new toys to show off. We pounce on the pages and read through them. They're on the edge of their seats as we discover whether they'll work or not. Some of it obviously looked better on the computer and is rejected; other bits are hilarious and work a treat. Once there's a verdict, they scuttle back into the writing room and hit the next scene.

We're working towards a complete read-through on Saturday afternoon. It's a stretch, as songs are coming in and out, the script is going back and forth, and actors are coming and going. We're trying to bed down which number we'll do for the penultimate drag performance. In the film it's 'Finally', but Simon wants to save this for the end of the show mega-mix. We talk about a revamped disco version of 'I've Never Been To Me', and try it out. It's not great, but it could work. I suggest a drag dramatisation of the Shelley Winters death scene from *The Poseidon Adventure,* set to a disco version of 'The Morning After'. Tick already mentions it in the show as something he does back in Sydney, so why not stage it? We try the song in a disco beat, and there's potential.

Spud looks weighed down by the massive workload. All the thousands of scraps of paper, ideas, key changes, and crazy requests by Simon seem to act like a myriad of tiny Lilliputian ropes, slowly dragging at him like Gulliver. He keeps sighing heavily and going back to the computer to bang together new sheet music and change keys and arrangements. Just as he's finished one, he has to change another. He's like a dormant geyser boiling beneath the surface and ready to blow. I don't want to be in the same suburb if he happens to go off.

The whirlwind continues until Saturday afternoon, when Garry arrives to listen to the read through. We've got as close to the final script as we can. We also have an underscore, and most of the songs arranged. As Spud shuffles his mass of scribbled arrangements into a semblance of order, Simon instructs him to have 'Girls Just Want to Have Fun' ready, as well as 'Do You Know the Way to San Jose', for a particular moment in the second act. A tiny puff of steam escapes the geyser, and I fear the worst, but after taking a moment Spud rolls his eyes and relents.

We gather around the piano for the read. It's so much more casual than the first workshop. We sit in a circle, scripts in hand, with none of the nerves associated with giving a performance. Everyone's excited and jokes are firing off all around me like cluster bombs. Garry is clearly loving his role of papa bear, presiding over his club, while Simon laughs animatedly with Phil's relentless gag festival. Even Spud, who peers out darkly from beneath his beaten brow, has a glint in his eye.

Before the whole afternoon is reduced to a total rabble, Simon calls us to order, and we begin the read.

What immediately strikes me is how funny it is. The best of Stephan's gags have been kept, and Phil and Allan have written more. The three lead characters seem warm, and their stories are compelling. The songs work beautifully with the dialogue, and even though they haven't been specifically written for the show, seem to help drive the story along. The underscore gives the scenes a real sense of depth and emotion. 'Both Sides, Now' has been flagged for one spot in the show, and I neither know nor particularly like it. When we get there I want to run and hide. Tony is as tentative with it as I am, and we leave it to Nick to hold the fort. Simon seems wedded to it, but I secretly hope it never makes it to rehearsals in a few months time.

With the odd exception, the read is a success. Garry looks happy as we turn over the last page and look up from the scripts. The whole room seems to have enjoyed going on the journey. The mood is buoyant, and we all seem to feel like this version of the script could take us to opening night and beyond. The gag fest sparks into life again as everyone gathers themselves up and begins to disband for the weekend.

After spending such an intense week together, we all feel very chummy and a little bewildered that we won't see each other again until rehearsals start.

I hug and kiss my way around the room on my way out, leaving Spud and Simon until last. I approach them and timidly stick my head into what seems to be a very intense conversation, offering my quick goodbye.

Simon jumps up and hugs me, and we share how positive we feel about the shape of the show. I turn to Spud and thrust out my hand, but I see he's in no mood for fond farewells. Sitting crossed-armed and immersed in a briny cloud of darkness, he gives me his worst union-boss scowl and tells me to get cracking on my singing lessons.

If there were an appropriate sound effect for this moment it would be a record player needle scraping across vinyl. This would be interrupted by the theme from *Jaws*.

Mouth gaping, I turn to Simon, whose expression exactly mirrors my own. 'Thanks for all your work this week, Jeremy,' or, 'See you at rehearsals in a couple of months for some more fun,' might have been more along the lines of what you'd expect from this parting encounter. But here I am tripping innocently through the sunlit forest, only to be leapt upon by the big bad wolf.

Feeling like I've just been punched in the guts, I grapple with a weak attempt to reassure him that my voice will be fine, that I have indeed gone back to singing lessons and will work my voice back into shape by the time rehearsals start. But Spud doesn't stop there. He begins a diatribe about how I haven't pulled my weight all week, haven't put in, and haven't committed to the singing, which has made his job all that much harder to hear what's working and what isn't.

Some dark creature begins to turn deep inside me. I grit my teeth against what it wants me to say, and I point out with a stiff politeness that I thought this week was a workshop where we were testing what could work theoretically for when we actually started rehearsing. He makes it clear that whatever it was for, he didn't get from me what he wanted.

Simon makes a weak effort to defend me, but the damage has already been done. We both stand in stunned, open-mouthed silence. With little else to say, I nod stiffly and storm out of the room, seething with hurt and anger. If I was nervous about my voice before, I'm now completely paranoid. Spud has simultaneously created in me a piercing desire to come to rehearsals brimming with a fit, confident voice and with an overwhelming self-consciousness that my singing will always disappoint him. Before becoming a part of this show I'd never doubted my voice at all. I'm aware of its limitations, but it's a nice voice that has stood me in good stead for many a night in the musical theatre.

I get to the car running the altercation over and over in my head. I try to understand what happened from Spud's perspective. Was I just in the way when the geyser finally blew? I fully expect my mobile to ring at any moment and hear Simon's voice smoothing things over, but it doesn't happen.

Hours later I'm still seething. The absence of a call from Simon makes me feel that maybe he thought Spud was right. Maybe I *had* taken the workshop too lightly.

At about nine thirty, Simon rings. He seems a little frantic. He'd been given the wrong phone number for me and had been trying to track me down all night. A little breathlessly, he assures me that when I approached them, Spud was in the middle of a melt down about how much needed to be done before rehearsals started, and that I got in the way. I accept that this may have motivated Spud's ferocity, but not necessarily the content of what he said.

With his uncanny people-skills working overtime, Simon soon makes me feel absolved, relieved, and a million times better. To be honest, just the fact that he called to offer his support was all I really needed. I feel Simon and I are on the same page heading into rehearsals, and we have each other's trust. I just can't know at this stage whether the egg can be unscrambled with Spud. Regardless of pre-existing misgivings, once you've been cast in a show surely the expectation must be that you should enjoy the support of the creative team as you head towards opening night together. This is what I hope for, and what will remain to be seen.

Chapter 7
A Cock in a Frock

For the first time in my life I commit heart and soul to singing lessons. Daily, I seal all doors and windows, and sneak glances over the fence to check there are no unsuspecting neighbours to offend before I warble away through my vocal exercises.

I trot out to Moonee Ponds twice a week to work with Roger, my passionate and rigorous singing teacher, who cajoles and bullies my voice back to its potential and beyond. I soon feel my voice slowly waking again, discover a range that has previously scared me, and begin to enjoy the sound of my singing once more. The process comes with the frustration of someone learning to walk again after a stroke. In theory, I understand what needs to be done, but keeping vertical when the crutches are thrown aside is terrifying and so often ends with me getting the wobbles and crashing to the ground. But my mind is fixed on day one of rehearsals, where I plan to change Spud's mind about my vocal ability.

Sydney soon beckons once more. Word comes through from the citadel that I have my first costume fitting. I'm very excited about this. Slipping on a costume for the first time is a wonderful way to engage with a show. Seeing yourself as the character you're about to play instantly makes you feel part of it. It reminds you that the wheels are turning somewhere, even though rehearsals haven't yet started. The Christmas elves are quietly toiling away in their caves somewhere, getting everything ready.

I get out of a cab in some far-reaching suburb in Sydney, and check the address on my care package. I navigate my way through a hidden doorway and up a set of creaky, wooden, Dickensian stairs. There's a security door with an intercom. I half expect Riff Raff from *The Rocky Horror Picture Show* to greet me. A cold wind sweeps up the staircase from the street. I press the intercom marked Anthony Phillips costumes.

'Yes?' says an indeterminate voice.

'Hi. It's Jeremy Stanford. I'm here for—'

There's a hard buzz and the lock clicks before I can finish. I push through the door, continuing up the old firetrap of a staircase.

At the top I find myself in an enormous warehouse space, filled with racks of half-finished costumes, fabric, giant hats, enormous coloured feathers, and staring mannequins. It's a place you could imagine coming to life at night. There's a vague smell of glue. An AM radio echoes distantly. Somehow, the tempest from the staircase doesn't make it this far into the building. All around the room the Christmas elves are hard at work sewing buttons and sleeves and sequins, and they look up from their toil as I enter. Once they've briefly regarded me, they forget I was ever there and go back to their labours.

I follow my instincts and wander into the fitting room. There I find Tim and Lizzy poring over sketches and fabric samples. I already feel slightly in awe of them, so I try to appear as cool as possible, but I'm the new boy in class today, and I'm sure I'm wearing it like a badge.

Tim beams at me and says, 'Hi, Sexy.'

Anthony Phillips hurries in like head Christmas elf, his face purple with stress, as if the show is going to open tomorrow night. He has armfuls of costumes for me to try on, and greets me only fleetingly. He gets me to strip to my undies and helps me into a corset.

Tim wears the smile of a man delighted to be watching this straight boy jump through a particularly unfamiliar hoop. The corset is black and boned, and Anthony pulls the ties squeezy tight. This is my first test of drag tolerance, and I'm determined to pass. I'm equal parts bewildered and amused.

I try on a pair of stilettos, just to get the right height for the frocks I'm about to try on. Once the corset is fitted and Anthony's established that I'm actually breathing, he helps me into my Opera House frock. It's a giant, Marie Antoinette outfit, which fills most of the room with its tent-like skirts. When certain levers are pulled, it will turn into the main two sails of the opera house. It has an enormous foam wig hat, which is about three feet high, and upon which a sailing ship teeters.

I can't stop laughing. It's outrageous. As nervous as I am in this outfit, I can't help being taken over by the feeling it gives me, which is that of some central European monarch unhinged by syphilis. I implore Tim to take a photo with my phone so I can send it straight to Annie. Once it's snapped and he returns my phone to me I go to send it, but I can't for the life of me think of an appropriate accompanying caption. In the end I write: !

I try on my 'I've Never Been To Me' frock. It's a fitted emerald green mermaid dress. It's so pretty that it raises 'oohs' and 'ahs' from far-away elves, who have snuck their heads around the corner to gawk.

I find myself mincing around the studio, posing shamelessly. This intensifies the delight in Tim's eyes. Anthony remains business-like, taking instructions from

Tim and Lizzy about adding and subtracting features to complete the dress. I don't like to mention it, but my feet are absolutely killing me in the shoes. I've been standing in them for fifteen minutes straight, and I wonder if I'm not wearing rabbit traps on my feet.

Once the frock is approved, I take everything off and remain shivering in nothing more than my undies and stilettos as I wait for the next outfit. Everyone is deep in conversation and seems to have momentarily forgotten me. With agonising relief, I quietly slip off my shoes, but get sprung doing so. Anthony wheels around and apologises, tells me to get dressed, that I'm finished.

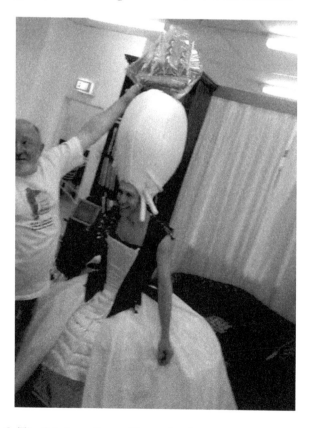

2. **The fabulous Opera House frock under construction.**

Just like that a cab is summoned, and I head back down the windy stairs.

The next stop is a moulding session for my head. To get around the problem of us getting in and out of drag make-up quickly, we'll be using masks. Drag make-up takes about an hour and a half to apply, so when we need to suddenly appear doing a drag number, we'll just slip on a mask instead. That's the idea, anyhow. I'm not sure anyone's proved it'll work yet, since it's a technique that has been developed for the show. Somehow, this next session will produce one of these masks.

A cab drops me at an industrial suburb out near the airport. It's the kind of area where I imagine murdered bodies are dumped. I take my life into my hands and dodge speeding lorries as I cross a ghastly motorway and enter a recently finished industrial estate. The enormous warehouses dwarf me as I follow the meticulous instructions on my care package to a large warehouse door, which looks more unused than used. Doubting I'm in the right place, I press the buzzer and am greeted by two men who look like members of the band Devo. They welcome me inside the cavernous workshop, which they don't seem to notice is freezing cold. Shelves line the walls, and there are numerous empty workbenches that look well used but are currently on leave.

The men tell me they make animatronics for film and TV creatures and monsters, and as they speak I notice a pile of lifelike monster heads on the bench next to the hand I'm leaning my weight on. I quickly withdraw my hand in case I'm bitten. If Anthony Phillip's costume warehouse came alive at night, I certainly wouldn't want to wander around *this* joint after dark.

The two Devo guys explain today's process to me as though they're reciting a safety drill on an aircraft. They crack funny but nerdy jokes, and finish each other's sentences. I'm in my best T-shirt, but they both wear crafty smocks that are covered in goo, and I begin to worry about the state I may be catching the plane home in.

They seat me in a salon chair and cover me with a plastic apron, before giving me two hand signals and asking me to repeat them so they know I've understood. One is for 'I'm okay', and the other is for 'I'm *not* okay'. I'm not getting a good feeling about this. I'm instructed to not move a muscle in my face during the procedure, as it will wreck the mask, and we'll have to start again. I make the gesture they've given me that means, 'I'm okay', as a lame attempt at humour, which they ignore as they bring large buckets of … I'm uncertain what … towards me.

I close my eyes and try to get comfortable as they smear my face with Vaseline. It feels cold and oily. They ask me my first, 'Are you okay?' and I make the sign. Then they entirely cover my face in dental paste, which smells minty and hardens with lightning speed. As it sets, I try to think pleasant thoughts, but the best I can come up with is feeling like my face is a giant tooth that's being cleaned. The dental paste makes its way into my mouth, and I feel it trickling down my throat. It's gritty and irritating, and I begin to imagine terrible thoughts such as I'm going to cough and ruin the whole process, or—even worse—vomit, then choke on it and die before they can get this whole shebang off me.

One of the Devo guys has left the room, and I hope it's not to get the large, sharp knife they use to decapitate their naïve hostages. The remaining guy cracks odd little jokes, and I have to resist reacting in case we have to start this process over. He asks again if I'm okay, and I give the sign.

Next they drape plaster bandages all over my face, which turns the hardened dental paste icy cold. I have two small straws sticking out of my nose to breathe with, and the powdery smell of plaster instantly takes me back to high school craft. Once the bandages are placed, they're secured, as my whole head is wrapped in bandages. My head soon feels like it's three times its natural size. I must look like a mummy from a fifties horror movie. Well, at least I'm not out of place here.

The whole construction, which feels like a diving bell on my head, stays on for about half an hour. Since I'm incapable of conversation, they leave me and go off to fool around with their other creatures. I can't hear much, but they seem to be having a good time doing *something* out in the workshop.

Eventually they return and begin to release me. They cut at the bandages and painstakingly peel it all off. When the contraption is removed there seems to be nothing to show for my troubles, only a strange, soccer-ball-like object, which somewhere inside contains my likeness. I guess they'll pour plaster into it and create an inanimate Jeremy, which will sit on a bench here, adding to their collection of creatures.

I clean myself up and go to the giant door that leads to the sane, outside world. On the way, I stumble upon a table that holds the collection of other heads made from the rest of the cast. My skin crawls. Everyone looks like a strange, cadaver version of themselves. It's all a little weird. Barely concealing my haste to leave, I politely thank the Devo guys and slip out into the warming sunshine, where I look forward to not shivering anymore. As I leave this freak show, I want to check that nothing has followed me out and could now be waiting in the bushes to slip unnoticed into the cab and eat me on the way to the airport.

It's been quite a day. With my consent I tried on my first dress and I was cloned. I've got lots to tell the kids.

Chapter 8
Drag Show

I've been trying to organise an excursion to a drag show for around six weeks, even though it's only around the corner, for God's sake. My dear friend Lily knows some of the girls there. She's promised that if I go with her she'll organise an introduction and arrange for me to scout around backstage, watch the make-up going on, and chat with the performers. She calls herself a queens' consult in preference to fag hag, which she thinks is misogynistic.

After the six weeks, we finally agree a mutually acceptable date—a date that turns out to be the night before I leave to go to Sydney for the start of rehearsals. I couldn't forgive myself if I'd turned up on day one having done no research at all, so I have to go. I've only ever seen one drag show, and it was through a cloud of alcohol after a *Buddy* show one night. I wouldn't say it's my hot choice for an evening's entertainment, but in the context of research I'm chomping at the bit to go.

As it's my last night with the family before I leave for

Sydney tomorrow, I prepare a slap-up meal before I go out, and we all sit down together with an air of formality and finality. I try to make it sink in—to Hunter at least—that Dad is going to go away to Sydney for a long time.

To children who have only ever known a stay-at-home-dad, this concept completely escapes them, and they move the conversation back to *SpongeBob SquarePants*.

In the middle of dinner the phone rings, and I get a breathless Ross Coleman on the line.

'Oh, thank God you're home,' he quakes. 'There's been a disaster!'

My stomach sinks. Simon has died in an accident. The producers have gone broke. They've cast Gary Sweet in my role.

'I'm cooking a goose for Simon, and my oven has broken down,' he says.

No one else I know is capable of a sentence like this. I don't quite know what to say or where this is leading.

'Can I come and cook it in your oven?'

This is, of course, no problem for me, but poor Annie, who doesn't eat game, may have issues.

'Hang on,' I say, and cup my hand around the phone. 'Ross wants to cook a goose in our oven. Is this okay with you?'

Annie nods, barely comprehending, and I jump back on the phone.

'Okay, but don't let it get out that I cooked your goose, Ross. Everyone will think that's how I got the job in the show.'

Ross, who is at a stress level way beyond responding to jokes, thanks me profusely and tells me frantically that he and Oleg have already made the chestnut stuffing, but something's gone wrong with the fucking oven. He hangs up saying one of them will arrive with the bird without delay.

As I'm leaving to go to the Newmarket Hotel for my drag night, Ross and Oleg arrive with a thank you bottle of wine and the already stuffed game on an enormous oven tray. They race in the door, like they have a patient who needs resuscitation, and plant the bird in the perfectly pre-warmed 180-degree oven.

'I can't thank you enough,' Ross says.

'Just as long as you leave me a taster,' I hint.

Choosing not to pick up the hint, Ross replies, 'You look nice. You going out?'

'I'm going to a drag show.'

Ross purses his lips with delight. He's always speculated on my sexuality, and the idea of me spending the night in a gay club positively thrills him.

'Don't do anything I wouldn't do,' he sings.

Fat chance, I think to myself. Is there *anything* he wouldn't do?

As I enter the hotel, I hit a solid wall of cigarette smoke. I'm sure some of this smoke has been wafting around this room since the seventies. A large proportion of it has settled on the walls and fittings. In the dimly lit haze I feel the drunken and avaricious eyes of a cackling hens night searching me as I collect my happy-hour pot from the bar.

There's no sign of Lily, and I'm forced to sit conspicuously alone. It takes them about thirty seconds to send out a scout, a carrot-haired woman in her mid-forties who is obviously the bride. She wears a costume shop version of a wedding dress and veil, with flashing neon lights woven into it. She drunkenly presses her elbows into the Formica table as she sits and flirtatiously insists I tell her how she and her friends know my face. I don't offer anything more than a friendly shrug, but she twigs I'm an actor and demands I tell her everything I've ever been in. Without going into specifics, I admit to being an actor and tell her I'm *very* famous.

'Well *we* don't know who you are!' she snaps, before tottering back to her friends, who cackle like banshees.

Oh, God, please get here soon, Lily.

Avoiding any further eye contact with anyone, I survey the room. It's remarkable only because it's managed to retain its seventies décor in this inner-city area, where any available venue has been snapped up by needle-eyed developers, desperate to gentrify all before them, and turn everything into a 'Murphy's Irish Pub'.

The room clearly hasn't had a lick of paint in decades, and at one end is a small homemade stage, which shares a backstage entrance with the route to the toilets. A few electric par can lights with coloured gels point unevenly inwards, and tables are spread neatly around the room. The tables all have salt and pepper shakers on them, which make me quake with trepidation at what kind of food would be offered up here.

The room is yet to fill, and besides my sweethearts— the hens—there are only a few tables of gay men and would-be girls with their trannie training wheels on.

Lily finally makes a commanding entrance, receiving fond greetings from bar staff and passing queens. She calls over Amanda Monroe, a glamorous drag who's approaching her senior years. They embrace, and she introduces me as an old friend who's about to do the *Priscilla* show in Sydney. I get a mixed reaction as Amanda pronounces *Priscilla* misogynistic and tired. I say we intend to freshen the old girl up, and the script we've finished with has a lot more heart in it than the film.

Amanda prides herself on being a philosopher of drag. She's very serious about it, and once you get her started it comes thick and fast. She tells me that, for her, it's all about challenging sexual stereotypes, demanding that the viewer look into what they see as normal sexuality, and getting their cage rattled. She relishes the idea of straight men getting a secret hard on as they watch a man perform for them dressed as a woman. It's something that confronts their idea of what sexuality is. She quotes someone I've never heard of who once said that a society that doesn't have drag queens doesn't fully understand itself—it only has a loose grasp on sexuality and its broader role in the community. She tells me early priests used to cross-dress in order to interpret how the gods wanted their society to behave. I nod mutely, trying to keep up with her earnest monologue. It's not what I expected. As much as it's fascinating and informative, my hunt tonight is really about personal accounts. What started you on this brave and unusual journey? What does it *feel* like for you? Which experiences have shaped your life? But I can't get a word in. Amanda's neatly rationalised her choice of lifestyle, but she seems to cloak it in philosophy, rather than exposing her true feelings.

She's clearly heading from mere drag queen into being a full transsexual (my carefully timed glances down to her breasts tell me they have been surgically enhanced), but I'm not getting the slightest clue as to *why* this lifestyle choice is so vital to her. I've heard other transsexuals say they're a man trapped in a woman's body, and the world doesn't feel right for them until they're living transgender. Maybe Amanda doesn't want me getting that close to her secrets.

She stops mid-sentence, like she's had a revelation, and asks if we do 'I Will Survive' in the show. I say we do. Suddenly, she's flushed. She leaps up exclaiming theatrically that *she* does 'I Will Survive' too, before she promises to show me how it's *really* done, and she charges backstage to dig out the outfit and the music.

Lily takes me backstage to meet Jess, who is responsible for the main show tonight. It's a version of *The Sound Of Music*, and Jess has written, directed, and sewn all the costumes. He's a squat, ordinary looking man who is just beginning to apply base make-up as I arrive. I introduce myself and ask if I could quiz him about all things drag. Although he's busy preparing to go on stage, I get the feeling talking about themselves and their art is a topic drag queens have little trouble with. He generously chats away as he applies a myriad of different colours to his face, and fixes on eyelashes the size of boogie boards.

He's more forthcoming in a personal way than Amanda. He tells me he's been doing drag since he was three. As a child he was into wearing his mother's shoes and clothes, and his mother and grandmother indulged him for years. Around eight, he stopped doing it. It wasn't until he was at school doing plays that his interest resurfaced. He went to an all-boy school, so he was handy in the school play as he always played the girl's roles. And so this continued into life. When he saw a drag show at The Imperial Hotel in Sydney, he was hooked. I imagine this is a story repeated time and time again.

As opposed to Amanda, for Jess it's all about releasing an inner persona through the dressing up. He says the clothes free something within him. He seems a determined but rather quiet man, someone you might misjudge as a push over. I await his metamorphosis.

He begins a rave about the origins of drag specifically related to Sydney. He tells me how Les Girls at Kings Cross was the beginning of it all. The girls there mimed to glamorous European recording stars while dressed in ornate outfits, and had the intention of actually coming off as women. Some even had the chop for greater legitimacy. As drag proliferated outside Les Girls, it evolved into being more of a cabaret performance with comedy involved, and the disguising of the man beneath the frock not being as crucial. In some quarters, it even became a kind of performance art with the costumes, music, and routines becoming quite avant-garde.

I become aware that Jess and Amanda haven't mentioned the word transvestite once. I'm certain this is a cultural thing. In Australia we have drag queens, but in England they have transvestites, and the two seem to be very different things. When I was last in London, I visited a mate who was playing a piano bar gig in a club in Soho. The bar was a renovated bomb shelter from the Second World War. To find it I had to locate a miniature, concealed doorway off a quiet lane, and navigate my way to the tiniest, stone stairwell, which lead down, down, down. I finally came to a room with a very low arched brick ceiling, like every classic picture I'd ever seen of a bomb shelter, but the club was loud, thick with smoke, dimly lit, and pulsing.

My friend was on a break from playing, and he rushed over. Beaming with delight, he told me it was cross-dressing night. I looked around, and sure enough every patron in the place was a man with a dress on, and they weren't disguising the fact they were men either. There were no wigs, they hadn't shaved after work, or even bothered changing out of their work shoes. Some of them even sported beards and moustaches. They'd literally just slipped out of their suits and into a dress, and were now nursing pints of warm beer as they chin-wagged in the din. One man approached me and in a deep, baritone voice, thick with a London accent, said, 'Hello. My name's Maria.' Bug-eyed, I smiled stiffly and turned to my friend and sang (from the classic tune from *West Side Story*) 'I've just met a man named Maria'.

We got chatting, and the man assured me he wasn't gay. No one in the bar was. They just liked dressing up as women and socialising like that. He told me he was married, as were most of the guys in the club, and that his wife knew all about his "Wednesday night frolics" and gave him her cautious blessing.

I'm sure there are many straight men who cross-dress in Australia too, but they're not drag queens. Drags tend to be gay and exist safely tucked away in the gay community, the way I'm sure the cross-dressers would find their own haunts as well. Drags are more theatrical. They seem to make a performance out of being a drag queen, rather than simply getting off on wearing women's clothes.

Jess banishes me as he puts on his final touches, and I take my seat for the first part of the evening's entertainment. The house lights dim, and Jess barrels onto the stage as a brassy and commanding woman. She calls the room to order, and no one dares challenge her robust authority. It's a bewildering transformation as Jess shows off his other self. She launches into a stand-up routine and pulls the bride who assaulted me earlier up from the hen's group and onto the stage. This previously loud and obnoxious woman is now completely eclipsed by Jess, who rakes in the laughs at her expense. Even the bride's timid attempts to get into the game act as fodder for Jess' razor sharp joke fest. Once she's finished with her, she sets the bride free and continues with the show. She introduces the first act. It's a mime to 'These Boots Are Made For Walkin', performed by a flaming red head. I'm blown away at how brilliantly she lip-syncs the song. It's as if she's actually singing it. Then a virginal Swedish dame enters and mimes to a bizarre song about a girl on top of a snowy mountain somewhere, which of course descends into ribald crudity. It's hilarious, and it brings the house down. I didn't realise drag was so funny.

Amanda enters dramatically and begins to perform 'I Will Survive'. It's a version I've never heard before, sung like a torch song with no disco beat at all. Amanda performs it like she's got a point to make. It's intense, dramatic, and very powerful. I think of Tony Sheldon. I wish he could see this. In the show, Bernadette has a speech about how important the technique is in getting the lip-sync just right. 'The vibrato of the Adam's apple, the quivering bottom lip.' Amanda is doing it all, and she strikes me as being a real life version of Bernadette. Even as I'm thinking this, Lily taps me on the arm and says she thinks Amanda may have had her tits done.

After a grand bow, Amanda sweeps off, and the house lights come up for intermission. The place has completely filled up. Jess mentioned before that the show was quite a success, but now I see that he was just being humble. The place is packed and rocking. The audience couldn't be more diverse. There are tables of gay men, gay women, hen's nights, a group of seemingly straight women, and a smattering of young drags. Amanda arrives, and I tell her I thought she was great. She takes the compliment flippantly and through a cloud of cigarette smoke.

I get a full beer for the second half of the show, which is *The Sound of Music*. Drag nuns enter and mime to 'How Do You Solve a Problem Like Maria'. It's hilarious, crude, and choreographed so cleverly that it makes the tiny stage seem somehow enormous. Beforehand, Jess had made no attempt to talk the show up at all, but it's well put together, and Lily and I piss ourselves laughing. The crowd roars all the way through. A lot of work has gone into it, and it's very entertaining.

When the interval comes I commit sacrilege by getting up to leave. Lily is stunned. I explain I'm leaving tomorrow for a few months, and I want to spend at least some of my last night in Melbourne with my wife. I ask her to explain this to Jess, and to send my thanks and congratulations.

The air outside smells like a crisp mountain breeze in comparison to the venue. I wander home, processing what I've just witnessed. It's inspired me for rehearsals on Monday, and I can't wait to get cracking.

When I walk in the door at home, the smell of cooked goose is intense. I'm immediately salivating. Annie shares with me the image of Simon, the dinner guest, sent to retrieve the cooked goose from our oven, and charged with the responsibility of traipsing back down the street on foot, balancing it on a silver platter. On Monday this forlorn waiter will turn into the master director before an eager cast. If only I had a photo to flash around.

I rush to the kitchen, hoping there'll be an offering of a small piece of goose flesh. I scour the room desperately, only to be disappointed. I'm shattered. You know who your friends are.

Chapter 9
She's Leaving Home, Bye Bye

If the phone rang to tell me the whole thing was a giant mistake and I didn't have to go, I'd be seriously relieved. It's Sunday, and I'm putting the finishing touches to my packing before I head to the airport for my flight to Sydney—and my semi-permanent life up there.

Perhaps subconsciously, I've packed lightly, even though I know I'm going away for months. Annie's taken the kids to a birthday party, and I'm rattling around the house on my own with a desperate sinking feeling in my guts. I've never been apart from my kids for longer than a few days, and the reality of leaving them chokes me up. I really, really don't want to go.

Annie and I have come up with a Plan A and a Plan B for the time I'm away. Plan A is for me to commute every two weekends to see the boys, and we'll wait and see how long the show goes on for. If it runs to February or March, maybe even April, then hopefully we'll all manage being apart, and my fortnightly trips will be enough of a presence to satisfy everyone. Plan B is panic stations. If we're not coping, she and the kids will move to Sydney and to hell with everything. I'm truly blessed with a wife who, having been in the business herself, gets the drill. She's happy to be absorbed into whatever plan works best at the time. I remind myself that thousands of divorced fathers only see their kids once a fortnight and they cope. Or do they? My dear friend Greg spent months apart from his kids last year. He tells me I'll get through it. There'll be dark, lonely times, but it's not as if I'm going off to war, for Christ's sake. I'm only an hour away.

I finish my packing with far too long to spare before the family gets back. I'm left alone to wander around the house with little to do but assess the wood pile and wonder if I've left enough split wood and kindling for Annie to manage the fire. I notice the flapping nature reed on the fence and wish I'd secured it properly yesterday. All the little jobs that are traditionally mine in the household swim through my mind, and I feel sick that they're now going to fall to Annie.

The phone rings. It's my Uncle Tony, whom I haven't spoken to in years, the guy who got me into the opera all those years ago. He's called to wish me good luck for the show. Miraculously, or maybe just through personal experience, he reads the tone in my voice and calls me on my reluctance to go. My misgivings flood out. I tell him I've made a conscious decision not to tour since the kids were born for exactly this reason. I want to see them grow up. There will always be another show, but what they and I miss out on by me being away is irreplaceable. They grow up so fast.

Tony finds exactly the words to reassure me that things will be fine. He and his family got through it, and so will I. This call couldn't have been better timed. It's as if it had been programmed by the producers to make sure I got to rehearsals on Monday morning. I thank Tony profusely and reshape the way I see the rest of my day.

The family drops me at the airport. One by one, I hug them goodbye, even though Ned, the little one, has fallen asleep on the way, so I miss out on any meaningful farewell from him. He will wake to find his dad has already gone. My heart breaks when I wave goodbye as they drive away. I take a deep breath and harden my heart to the bustling and impersonal experience of the airport.

My accommodation at Coogee Beach is all that I had hoped for. It's in the hub of the shopping centre, minutes from the beach. As I pay the cabby and roll my enormous suitcase across the street to the hotel, I'm already ticking boxes: there's a good cafe, a handy supermarket, a bank, a video shop.

After my royal greeting from the staff, I dump my bags in my room and assess the view of the beach from my balcony. I wander the apartment, familiarising myself with all the goodies.

After a time of just plumbing the bob, I decide to launch into the job of getting myself set up for the immediate future: unpacking, getting food in, sorting my internet connection, checking bus routes and timetables to get to work, and exploring my new 'hood. I'm on the phone to Annie every ten minutes, and I have a burning desire to kiss my kids.

As I wander around the streets, I feel my focus closing in around me, as I prepare to immerse myself in rehearsals. The job in front of me is enormous.

For the first time in six years I'm not beholden to children when I plan my every moment of the day, and I have a whole new city as my playground. I check myself into a hotel of denial. Until the show is up and running, I plan to do little else but work.

Chapter 10
The Marathon Begins
Rehearsals: Week 1

I've prepared my briefcase with all necessary "first day of school" items: sharpened pencils, notepads, tape recorder with fresh batteries, cut lunch, and my script, with all my lines highlighted. With Rolex precision, I make my way to the bus stop, knowing exactly what time it will arrive and when it will deposit me at rehearsals. I wait with waning optimism for a bus that has clearly been cancelled. I catch the next bus, but I'm now officially running late.

I arrive at the Brent Street Studios, where we'll be rehearsing. This is a Sydney institution, which essentially trains performers from the age of nappies, right up to High School Certificate aged kids. On any given day you can see flocks of perfectly poised children, jazz-running their way to their next tap, ballet, or modern class, their perfectly quaffed mothers whispering their goodbyes, their own dashed hopes and dreams of the stage now rolled up in the next generation of the family.

The studios sit smack in the middle of Moore Park,

which is a suburb on the way to somewhere else. The entrance to the building is inviting enough, perhaps an attempt to convince hopeful parents that the entertainment industry isn't that bad and won't gobble their little angels alive.

I find A4 notices sticky taped to a wall in the foyer directing me to "PRISCILLA REHEARSALS". I snake my way through the building following the signs. It's like some incredible catacomb with fading paint and the smell of pigeon shit. Corridors lead off in all directions like an M.C. Escher painting, and I thank God I'm following signs. I wonder at what this place used to be with its countless enormous spaces and huge, heavy rolling doors. In its heyday, what kind of industry would have needed this much space? NASA? Only the arts would put up with the squalor it presents now.

Several staircases and bewildering corridors later, I start doubting I'll ever find my way out. Maybe I should be leaving a trail of breadcrumbs. Finally, I make my way onto the fourth floor and through the sliding steel door to our rehearsal room.

It's enormous. The floor is worn out linoleum, and one wall is entirely made up of rain stained louvered windows. The roof sags with hessian fabric, and mirrors completely line two other walls. A cold breeze blowing in from the industrial street below brings dust in with it, and I instantly feel grimy.

The room is vacant, so I continue through to the offices and green room out the back. I can hear the rumble of voices as I approach, and I get a little tickle of excitement and nervousness. I round the corner and find the company all milling. Kath, our 'pin-up' of a stage manager, is ushering everyone into the rehearsal room. She's relieved I've finally arrived, and I blame the Sydney bus service for my tardiness.

Scores of chairs have been set up facing an electric keyboard in front of the louvered windows. As we file in,

I hug the few members of the cast I already know or have previously met, and then I head over to Simon, who's beaming to all and sundry. We greet warmly and swap jokes about the now famous goose from Saturday night. Ross smiles shyly and then roars with laughter. I shake Spud's hand, and he flashes me a smile. It's the first time I've seen him since the spray he gave me at the second workshop, and he seems quite affable. Maybe all is forgiven. I feel heartened.

I take a seat at the front of the room with Tony and Daniel. Unlike a play where all the actors sit around the table for the first read through, in a musical, usually the principals sit at the front facing the creative team, and the ensemble sits behind. It's a crazy kind of 'billing' pecking order.

Simon interrupts the loud rumbling of chat, and once everyone is quiet he beams at us and says, 'Isn't this exciting? We're all going to be *very* famous.'

Everyone collapses with laughter, before Tony Sheldon quips, 'Yeah, just like the *Mamma Mia*! cast.'

Simon begins proceedings with a short introduction of everyone in the room, starting with the creative team, then the crew, and then the producers. Incredibly, he remembers everyone's names. There must be sixty people in the room. When he gets to the cast, he tires and asks us to do it ourselves.

'It's easy,' he says. 'You just stand up and say, for example,' he picks me out of the crowd, 'hi, I'm Jeremy Stanford, and I'm an alcoholic.'

I stand and say, 'Hi, I'm Jeremy Stanford, and I'm an alcoholic.'

The mantle gets passed around. People stand and introduce themselves. Most have a witty quip to accompany their introduction: 'Hi, I'm Michael, and I'm terrified.' There's a palpable sense of nervous excitement bristling through the room. Simon closes off by saying he can't wait to get to work on the show, and that although it's going to be hard work we'll all have a lot of fun.

Then it's Spud's turn. He attacks his speech like a drill sergeant, warning us that the producers have spent *a lot of money* getting this show to this stage. He says they've been incredibly generous with their cash, and it's time to make sure it becomes a success.

'The creative team have spent six months working their arses off to make this thing happen, and the good news for them is, now it's *your* turn. If this show bombs,' he warns, 'it'll put Australian musical theatre back five years. Not only that, but the buck stops with Simon. We'll all get on with our lives, but for Simon it'll ruin him.'

We look over to Simon, who is grimacing comically, like this is the first time he'd contemplated such a thought.

'Thanks, Spud,' he says, resisting an anxious giggle.

'So I want to see nothing less than a one hundred percent commitment from all of you over the next six weeks,' Spud continues.

I look around the room at the excited, eager expressions on the faces of this collection of talented people, the cream of the crop from the auditions, and I wonder who on earth he's talking to. As if anyone is going to let this opportunity slip. As if there's a single leaner in the room.

With our first read through being on Thursday, he tells us we'll be learning the entire musical score for the show, harmonies and all, before then. Some arrangements aren't quite finished yet, so he'll be in and out finishing things, and at times his assistant Dave will hold the fort.

We begin with a vocal warm up, which fortunately I take extremely seriously, as at the end of it Spud gives us all a bollocking about how too many of us slacked off on it. I thank God my conscience is clear.

First up is 'Downtown', the opening number of the show. I don't sing in it, so I gratefully take the first half hour off. There are only a handful of us not in the song, so we retire to the green room, which is populated with an array of vinyl couches from the seventies, and enough coffee making facilities to caffeinate an army. Without such a huge throng to negotiate, I work the room more comfortably.

I meet up with Trevor Ashley, who was dressed as his drag character last time I saw him, so effectively it's our first meeting. If some drags need their wig, make-up and frock to unleash their personality this certainly isn't the case with Trevor. The producers were desperate to include at least two members of the drag community in the show, not for window dressing but because they really wanted the community to be involved. Regardless of their intentions, Trevor is definitely not window dressing as he has an amazing voice and is brimming with talents as a writer, director, actor, and musician in his own right. He has a permanent Luna Park smile on his face, and is as big-hearted with his attentions to others as with his willingness to talk about himself. I imagine him as equal parts generously loving and ferociously bitchy. Every second sentence is punctuated with a cackle reminiscent of the geese that fought over my stale bread on Lake Rotorua. I confide my nervousness about getting into drag, and my ability to perform it convincingly.

'Dahhhhhhhling,' he assures me, 'I'll look after you. We'll go down to the Imperial, and I'll introduce you to Mitzi Macintosh.' Each sentence is slightly elongated, as though it's being sung. 'You'll be fine, don't you worry about a thing.'

And I believe him. I feel like I'm going straight to 'the source'.

Tony, Daniel and I get some time to bond. I don't want to contrive it, but it's so important that the three of us click. Having worked with Tony in the workshops I know we'll be fine. He's the consummate professional and approaches everything with good cheer and hard work. Daniel is still a mystery to me. This morning he is understandably nervous. He confides that he'd been having panic attacks last week about beginning work today. Why wouldn't he? I've got a lot more shows than him under my belt, and I'm still terrified.

He hasn't finished *Dusty* yet. Tonight he heads back to Adelaide for closing night, so we won't have him again until Wednesday.

Michael Caton has joined the cast to play Bob. Although Billy Brown was rumoured to be playing it, somehow Michael has landed the role.

Soon Tony and I are called in to learn 'Don't Leave Me This Way', the funeral song. It's an ensemble song, but Tony takes the lead at the beginning. Sheet music is handed out, and Spud starts to teach it. I scour my parts to see how high I'm going to have to sing. My stomach knots as I see nothing but high notes. Tony and I turn to each other and grimace. True to my word though, I belt it out as best as I can, knowing I won't be able to do too much more of this before my voice is in rags.

Once we finish the song Spud calls a break, but he asks me to join him at the piano. My heart sinks. I'm terrified I'm going to get another spray, but I know I sang my guts out in the last session. I arrive at the piano with my heart in my mouth.

'I want you to hear the arrangement for 'Say A Little Prayer',' he says.

3. Rehearsals day one. Spud leads us through 'Don't Leave Me This Way'.

Suddenly I notice he's brimming with excitement.

'It took me ages to come up with a way to arrange it that suits your voice and would work in the show, but I think I've got it. Have a listen.'

He's practically shaking as he hands me the sheet music and hits play on the CD player. I'm stunned and relieved. He encourages me to gently sing along with it. It's a beautiful, delicate arrangement, which is perfect for my voice. It's sparse, but has enough instrumentation to give it a mournful beauty. As I sing, I can see how proud he is of what he's done, and so he should be. When the song finishes we share a nod, and I tell him I think it's beautiful, that it will be a truly touching moment in the show.

In the break I meet David Page. He's playing Jimmy, the indigenous man we bump into in the outback scene. It's such a coup to have him in the show, and I'm honoured to work with him.

Simon and the rest of the creative team have all vanished. Spud is running the show now, and it seems he will be until the whole score is learnt. As the day progresses, we plough our way through song after song. Everything is very high for Tony and me, and we're both getting paler and paler as the day drags on. We're also singing far more in the show than we thought we would be, and all of it is at the top of our ranges. Tony confides that he feels like the least talented person in the room. I don't know how to respond to that besides giggling at how ludicrous the thought is, but in a funny way he's hit the nail on the head. I feel exactly the same.

The final task for the day is to sing through all we've learned so far. Clutching sheet music, we bash it out as best we can. And then that's it. We're dismissed. First day of rehearsal over and out.

I'm so relieved to be going home. I weave my way out of the building, my head throbbing with fatigue. I can't wait to call Annie and speak to the kids. I'm already missing them dreadfully, and all I want to do is go home to Melbourne. I've set myself a regime of homework and exercise while I'm rehearsing, so once I get back to the Medina I have a swim, look at what we did today, and then cook dinner. By the time that's done, it's bedtime. The whole deal will start again tomorrow.

It's Tuesday and the principles' songs are scheduled for today. I'm terrified they'll all be as high as the ensemble numbers and therefore be unsingable for me.

I meet Tony as I arrive, and I ask how his voice is doing. He rolls his eyes. 'Not good.' He tells me he'd rung his mother, Toni Lamond, last night, freaking out about the keys being too high. She kept telling him, 'Say something! Say something!' He vows to have a chat with Spud about it today. I'm relieved it'll be him, not me.

Nick Hardcastle is filling in for Daniel today while Daniel's in Adelaide, and he stays with us as the ensemble is shuffled off to the music room to drill harmonies. 'Both Sides Now' has made it into the show, even after it went so badly at the second workshop. To our enormous relief, Spud has worked miracles with the arrangement. It's in a lower key for a start, but he's also put it into three-part harmony and given us all parts we can reach.

We move onto 'We Belong'. Spud says he's worried the song is now permanently associated with *Bridget Jones*. I don't have a clue what he's talking about as I haven't seen the film, but he's completely reworked the arrangement, and it is now a big, choral epic of a song. Again, it's in a better key and the harmony I'm given is good for me. I feel the blood returning to my body.

After lunch the entire cast gathers to sing through the whole show. It's like a joke. We only started learning this monster yesterday, and now we're singing through the thing from start to finish, complete with harmonies. A lot of the songs have backing tracks, and Spud plays along with them. The end result is that it doesn't sound that far off being like a real performance. I find that my solo numbers are all in a good key to sing, but my parts in the group numbers are still far too high.

When we reach the end, we're all stunned at how good it sounds for day two. The ensemble is dismissed, and the three leads stay to polish the principles' numbers. My voice is ragged, and I really, really want to call it a day.

On the break, I spy Tony take Spud aside. I hope he works the Sheldon magic on him. When the confab breaks up, Tony makes a beeline for me and says gravely, 'He wouldn't budge an inch.' We're both a little stunned, as we know we can't sing way above our ranges for eight shows a week. Our voices will be shot in a matter of days.

When we return after the break, I've got bugger all voice left. We sing through our songs a couple of times, but I'm getting seriously panicked about blowing my voice for tomorrow. Just as I'm about to raise my hand to pull the plug, Spud lets us off the hook. Day two finishes just like day one, with me bolting for the door.

My heart bleeds for poor Nick, who filled in for Daniel yesterday. It's Wednesday, and he's relegated back to the ensemble. The disappointment is barely concealed on his face. Understudying must be one of the most thankless jobs in show business. If ever I have an understudy in a show I always make sure they get at least a few shows on. There has to be a reward for all their work. Once they're secure with what they're doing in the role I quietly approach them and ask them if they'd like to go on. It might not be technically the right thing to do, but it's only fair.

Daniel finished in *Dusty* last night and has had three hours sleep. He's wired, though. He throws himself into learning what he missed out on, picking up his parts effortlessly. When I call him a bastard for being so quick, he mumbles humbly that he has a photographic memory. Our songs sound pretty, and the three of us put everything we've got into them. I'm still nursing my voice though, making sure I have something left for the rest of the week.

At lunchtime, gossip is rife. One story is that we're the top-selling show, before opening, of any show in Australian history. Another is that after the press launch, the producers kicked in another three million dollars. The last, and the best, is that the wardrobe department is having trouble finishing the feather headpieces because of the Bird flu epidemic.

After lunch, Ross arrives to choreograph 'Downtown'. He seems nervous. Physically shaking, he sits before the gathered ensemble and introduces how he likes to work. He describes his method as organic. He takes his movement from the individuals in the number, each body suggesting their own unique passage in space. The dancers look inspired.

We listen to the music and Ross' brain ticks over. His assistant, Andrew, sits to attention next to him, waiting for Ross to provide him with the germ of an idea, which he will then teach to the group. They're an amazingly close team. The dancers throw in ideas, and the song begins to take shape. As a non-dancer, I'm astounded how a dancer can watch a head-spinningly fast step and instantly repeat it. For me, learning choreography is like being asked to deliver a speech in Japanese. I need time to find each syllable as it crosses my tongue, and must slowly learn how to string this collection of unfamiliar sounds together with any sense of finesse.

Towards the end of the session Simon's assistant, Dean, gets a call. Simon is on his way to see what we've done. Ross is furious. He's run out of inspiration for the day and desperately wants to go home right now. He knows if Simon appears he'll want to adjust things, and Ross doesn't have the energy. He instructs Dean to tell Simon we've all gone home, and he dismisses us.

It's Thursday morning, and I drag myself out of bed. I've been awake all night with yobbos and garbage trucks and restless thoughts of my family. My voice is shot, and I'm so homesick for the kids that my head throbs.

Today has been called 'day one', the first read through. Strangely, I'm incredibly nervous. Fighting my homesickness and my nerves, I arrive at rehearsals to be confronted by photographers and TV cameras. Thankfully, none of them want anything to do with me. It's Michael Caton they really want, and he dashes past me trying to take cover, playing a futile game of hide and seek with them.

As I look around, it dawns on me that 'day one' has become a circus. Unlike the 'first read-throughs' I remember where it's a nice 'sit around the table and read the script' affair, we have the press, the producers, the creative team, and a bunch of hangeronerers like I've never seen in my life, all filing in like it's Ramadan at a mosque. Have things changed so much since I've been away? The audience seating that's been erected would be the envy of any self-respecting fringe festival show. The guests, half of whom are already seated and waiting expectantly, will sit facing us for the read. I bloody hope they're charging admittance. TV presenter Richard Wilkins roams the place doing perky grabs for morning television.

I look down at what I'm wearing. No one has warned me our first read is to be broadcast on national TV, and I'm in my dirty cargos and rehearsal shirt. Given a hint of this hype I'd at least have worn a nice shirt. What will Mum think?

Kath wrangles everyone into their appropriate positions, audience into their seats, the cast into theirs. Tony, Dan, and I sit central, surrounded by the other leads, and then the ensemble. The audience settles, and I see for the first time how many there are. I don't know most of them, and wonder if half of them haven't booked through Ticketmaster.

Simon steps forward and welcomes everyone. I always relax when he has the floor, and eagerly await his speeches. He thanks Tony and me for being the only surviving members of the original workshops, saying that I was twenty-five and Tony thirty-five when it all began. He goes on to acknowledge the designers, writers and producers who have contributed to getting the show this far, singling out Spud as being amazing.

Then, the jewel in the crown of any 'first day', we get to look at the set. The designer, Brian Thomson, shyly takes the floor and with a scale model of the set, complete with tiny backdrops that fly in and out, he talks us through how the show will look. He drives Priscilla, the bus, through the tiny stage, like a child playing with toy cars, proudly demonstrating all the things it will do. It goes forward and backward and turns three hundred and sixty degrees. It even changes colour. The side flips up so the audience can see inside. The wheels turn. It has elevators to raise the actors up onto the roof, and it's about three metres short of a real life bus.

The wow factor is intense. Everyone 'oohs' and 'ahhs'.

Then we get a slide show of the costumes. They are mind blowing. A rumour I heard was that there's one headpiece that cost $40,000 to make.

After everyone is suitably dazzled by the designers' display, it's the cast's turn to step up to the plate. It occurs to me why we've worked so hard getting all the songs learnt. This is a semi-showing where the nuts and bolts of this new piece of theatre will be unveiled. The producers want to see how their development money has been spent. Now I feel under enormous pressure. Not only are the TV cameras on the prowl, but the success or failure of this reading will make its way out into the real world in a very tangible way. There's no room for failure here. Producers are perched above, hawkishly watching their investment mature. Unproductive actors will be swooped on, carried to the side of the mountain, and dropped into the yawning ravine.

As the read begins I feel slightly resentful, inhibited, and quite nervous. Thankfully the first few minutes of the show for me are mute, and I can gather myself. We sing 'Downtown' followed by 'Never Been to Me', where I mime to Danielle singing the song. Then my first scene begins. I quickly realise I don't have Tick back yet. I can't find his voice or the feeling he gives me. I feel a note of panic. I withdraw slightly, burying my face in the script. Next to me, Tony is having no trouble with Bernadette, effortlessly belting out his lines. Dan follows Tony's lead, making a performance out of this, rather than just a 'read'. I still find myself thinking that we shouldn't have to be doing this!

As the read continues, I feel Tick returning. Soon we're approaching my solo song, 'Say A Little Prayer', and I become very nervous. I don't even know how to sing it yet, but I'm expected to perform it. I feel my voice tighten up, and I'm disappointed with how it sounds.

The bonus of performing the 'read' is we get an impression of how funny it is. The cast is buoyed by how much the audience laughs, and it genuinely feeds the playing of it.

When we finish, the audience scatters, leaving us to scratch our heads as to what the hell that was all about. To be honest, I did get a lot out of hearing the reaction of the crowd. I get a few warm handshakes from various producers, which is heartening, but I want to remind them that none of us know what the hell we're doing yet.

I head to the park for lunch and sanctuary. It's week one, but the pressure is intense. Maybe I've been away too long and have forgotten how it feels.

Without so much as a word about how bizarre the morning was, the afternoon begins with choreography. Now the 'read' is over, rehearsals begin in earnest. We pick up where we left off with 'Downtown'.

Simon watches what we did yesterday and instantly calls for changes. Ross is wary. So is Spud. One of the changes means taking four bars out of an instrumental break, which means a long night for Spud, and completely rearranging and re-recording the backing track. Spud gives Simon a withering look, which Simon simply absorbs, before insisting it must be done. After a momentary standoff, he gets his way and the rehearsal continues.

Ross invents a kind of shorthand for the dancers to describe the movements he's creating. He names the first set piece, "Fuck You", which is then followed by "Hernia". The dancers soon catch on to his eccentric turn of phrase and know exactly what he means when he asks them to return to "Furtive Fingering", "Blow Up Dolls", "Dog Shit", or "Mobile Phone". When they're run together, the movements make up the choreography that is 'Downtown'. I feel so proud of him as I witness these wonderful dancers awaken to Ross' rare brilliance.

After work I head to Nick's place for dinner. He's generously offered to cook dinner for the lonely guy. A couple of bottles of wine and a good chat ease my homesickness and my anxiety about the rehearsals. It's not great for my voice though, and I go to work on Friday still feeling vocally ragged.

After a recap of 'Downtown', we move on to 'Don't Leave Me This Way', the funeral number. Ross is clearly expected to do what Spud did in the first three days of rehearsal and choreograph the entire show in the next few days. It's a gargantuan task because you can't just write it down and then hand it out to learn. It has to be created and taught on the floor. Going from one number straight into another is clearly stressing him out. He theatrically presses the back of his hand to his forehead and says he's not a machine.

During the break, Trevor takes me aside and asks if I'm going to 'tuck' during the show. I can only imagine what this is and what it entails. With great earnestness, he recommends I spend the whole show 'tucked' as it will get rid of everything once and for all, and I won't have to worry about my bits getting in the way. Part of me is appalled. He's suggesting I get rid of what most men do their utmost to enhance, but then my mind flashes back to the auditions in Melbourne where I was painfully aware of a rather unseemly bulge in my dress. I can't be having that in the show. He talks me through the whole grisly process, explaining that you use a certain pair of Bonds briefs to shift the penis and scrotum up under the underside of the crotch, and then you hold it in place with a G-string. He assures me that it doesn't hurt unless you use a thong-type support. I'm not sure I clearly understand everything, and he promises to bring in the said apparatus tomorrow and show me. By the end of the conversation I'm convinced this will be my future, eight shows a week, with my poor old penis strapped to within an inch of its life in a place where the sun really, really never shines.

Saturday, and I've been given the morning off. It's a chance to catch my breath, as the week so far has felt enormous. When I arrive at rehearsals in the afternoon, I find out that Ross has also had the morning off, though not scheduled. 'Colemanitis', I'm told. The stress of the week has got to him, too.

Tony, Dan, and I work scenes with Simon. I feel more at home with this and find it a lot of fun. Simon gives us a basic blocking of the scene, and we play with it till it works. The scene involves Felicia singing a send-up version of 'Go West', involving copious amounts of alcohol. Spud informs us that we can't use the 'Go West' melody for this spoof of the song because the Village People's lawyer won't allow us to change the lyrics and is appalled we'd even think of doing such a thing. The rights have been withheld. We're going to have to think of something else for this moment.

It's a lonely, quiet rehearsal room on a Saturday

afternoon with no ensemble present. Four floors below, a garbage truck can be heard tipping large bins. At one point in a scene, Tony—playing Bernadette—lets out a long queenie scream, 'Aghhhhhh!' in response to Adam's constant teasing. Suddenly from way below in the laneway, a lone voice exactly echoes Tony's scream, with the same tone and intonation. We all stop dead and collapse laughing. It reminds us that the world is still turning outside, and that our boisterous rehearsals are easily overheard from the street. Tony puts his hands on his hips and yells back, 'How dare you! I'll come down there and hit you with my Helpmann Award!'

We work the scene in which we sing 'Both Sides Now'. After tossing the song around and trying different versions, Simon decides to cut a verse and therefore create a key change. Behind the piano, Spud goes grey. Simon notices this and sheepishly asks if it's possible. Spud shakes his head gravely and says, 'This is major, major, major.' It means re-recording the entire opera aria, which follows in a different key, orchestra, vocals and all. Simon goes quiet. Everything goes quiet. The rehearsal stops as the two men look down at the pages in front of them, studying their scripts and wishing this impasse would go away. Spud's mood is palpable. Simon summons the courage to say that this is the only way it's going to work. I wander to the far side of the room. I feel like I'm tiptoeing away from a live bomb, which has a feather trip switch. The men confer at length, and finally Spud graciously concedes Simon's right and agrees to the change.

Once the decision's made, all the air has gone out of the rehearsal room. It's late in the afternoon, and everyone is shot. I tremble with the notion that we may be released for the weekend, and I can taste the beer I'm about to devour. Simon asks us to run the scene once more, and then we quit for the day.

And that's it—week one over. We've learnt so much,

but have so much yet to learn. I head out into the late afternoon greyness, a little bewildered about what to do with my weekend freedom.

Chapter 11
Rehearsals: Week Two

Today, I'm a man possessed. Part of my gusto can be attributed to having played football yesterday. This is one of the great gifts of revitalisation given to mankind. A bunch of actors, artists, and assorted fanatics religiously assemble at a dishevelled oval in Alexandria Park every Sunday morning to kick the 'pill'. It's the Sydney chapter of a gang of madmen I kick with in Melbourne. Don't get me wrong; we don't play a game, as that would be far too physical. We do what's called circle work, and the ball travels clockwise around the oval, each player kicking or hand-balling to the next, *as if* we're playing a game. Almost everyone is far too old and injured to be a respectable athlete, but it's hilarious in its earnestness, as each of us relives his past glory days of football heroics. I arrive in a state of stressed panic from the week's pressure, and leave with the gaze of a Buddha having walked the seven steps to Nirvana. In two hours of footy, I run off all the campery and stress of *Priscilla*. Subsequently, I arrive at work a new man. Everyone is assembled waiting for Ross Partington, an esteemed osteopath, to deliver a speech about the challenges of working in high heels—so I'm straight out of footy boots and into stilettos.

Ross Partington's emaciated frame sweeps into the room late. He launches into an impassioned and exacting PowerPoint display, depicting in forensic detail what happens to the body whilst wearing high heels. It's hair-raising and has the shock value of road trauma. So animated is he in his rapid-fire delivery, that soon he literally begins to foam at the mouth. Not only is it hard to follow the science he's espousing, but his mad professor manner is beginning to crack most of us up. Nervous stage management try to hush our giggles with stern looks, but even they find the lecture to be heading into the territory of a crazed comedy routine. As Ross approaches his allotted hour, Kath is forced to pipe up that he has only a few minutes left and perhaps he should demonstrate some useful warm-up exercises to the cast. For a moment he looks as if he'll turn on her like a rabid dog, but then, resisting that urge, he instead chooses to react like a chastised child, grumbling that there's no point doing exercises if we don't know what is happening to the body.

Grudgingly, he takes us through some agonising exercises to strengthen the appropriate muscles and so spare us from osteoarthritis in our old age. We slip into stilettos and spend a painful fifteen minutes striding around the rehearsal room on tiptoes, as he exacts his revenge on our mirth and impatience.

When rehearsals finally begin, Tony and I are taken aside to help Spud solve the terrible key change car accident from Saturday. Spud looks as if he's spent all weekend on it, but the results are reassuring. The scene now works.

'Go West' is chalked in for today. We broke the back of this musically at the second workshop, so now we just have to choreograph it—but Ross is clearly not himself. He's edgy and nervous, and his usual muse has deserted him. He stands before us bereft of ideas. The ensemble begins to share doubting looks. For those who haven't worked with him, Ross' method is easy to mistrust. It looks like he doesn't know what he's doing until the dance is completed, and then suddenly you're in the middle of the Coleman magic. But the magic is not coming.

He keeps squeezing the bridge of his nose with his fingers and repeating, 'I don't know. I just don't know.' I try to help him out by offering suggestions, but I feel like I'm annoying him. Tony whispers to me that Ross is having trouble because aside from the speed he's forced to work at, the songs are covers and have no real narrative, so he's finding it hard to find the motivation for the choreography. The day goes very slowly as the song very gradually takes shape. It's like pulling teeth, and the ensemble are restless and frustrated.

Tuesday begins with a shoe fitting. At this stage they're not much more than pieces of fabric covered with scribbled lines, which are snipped and pinned in order to get my exact measurements. One pair of shoes will be high-heeled Blundstones, and the others are enormous high-heeled thongs.

In rehearsals we make a start on 'I Will Survive', mostly to time a costume quick-change. While Bernadette mimes the first part of the song, Felicia and Tick disappear behind the bus to change into the Gumby outfits. We discover we have exactly ten seconds to get off stage, out of our costumes, into new shoes, clothes, make-up mask and an enormous hat, and be back on stage for our cue. It's just not going to happen. We play with leaving the song earlier to give us more time—twenty seconds. Simon nods, satisfied. 'This can be done,' he says. I can't believe my ears.

While we go off to drill harmonies, the ensemble

reluctantly continues work on 'Go West'. They look grave as they head into what is likely to be another frustrating session with Ross.

Spud is strangely jovial, despite having stayed up until four this morning re-doing 'Go West'. Simon and Ross had requested changes to it, and he has cheerfully complied. The workload must be staggering for Spud at the moment.

In the afternoon we finish 'Don't Leave Me This Way'. After struggling through the rest of 'Go West', Ross seems to enjoy this number, and the song is quickly finished.

Wednesday comes, and the show's starting to feel like the choreography session that never ends. Number after number keeps coming at us. I can't imagine how the ensemble can learn it all. They keep commenting to me about how much Tony, Dan and I have to cope with, but I wouldn't swap with them for a second. Today we work 'I Love The Night Life', which is in a scene in The Palace Hotel. Genevieve Lemon gets to step out of the ensemble and strut her stuff. She plays a terrible country mullet who reacts to the queens as they enter the pub in full drag. It's an hilarious scene, and Gen extracts every possible laugh from it. Infuriating really that Tony, Dan, and I are on stage all bloody night and Gen steals the show in five minutes flat.

I choose to rehearse in heels today, which is agonising and also slows me down. My respect for women soars as the pain in my feet goes from unbearable to just plain numb.

When the session ends, Ross looks more fragile than ever. He has to fly to Melbourne to do a master class with Chita Rivera tomorrow. He's freaking out about it, as the number that's been chosen, without his consultation, is *All That Jazz*. For a start, it's a classic Bob Fosse routine, and Ross' work has always been compared to his, but Ross doesn't like the song either. He's agonising over whether to cancel or not. After the exhausting week he's had, this is the last thing he needs.

Without Ross, Thursday is spent mostly on scenes. Most of the time is devoted to blocking, and the logistics of getting furniture on and off the revolve. Little time is spent on any character work, so it all feels rather technical. Strangely though, it's a relief as the pressure is off for a moment.

I've organised to meet Garry McQuinn at the Newtown Hotel tonight, where he'll introduce me to Cindy Pastel, the drag queen Tick is loosely based on. He's doing his show there, so I can kill two birds with one stone and both see a drag show and meet Cindy. I wonder what kind of reception I'll get from him. As I get out of the cab my phone rings.

'Jezza, I'm so sorry to do this to you, mate, but I'm in a restaurant in the Cross and the main meal hasn't come yet.' It's Garry, standing me up. I let him off the hook, and nervously ask if I'm going to get a knife between the shoulder blades from Cindy. Garry assures me that Ritchie/Cindy is absolutely lovely and is looking forward to meeting me.

I approach the hotel with a tiny sense of foreboding. Gay bars are not what you'd call my usual haunt, and I don't fancy nursing a beer at the bar on my own for too long. When I arrive, it strikes me what a different scene it is in Sydney as opposed to Melbourne. The pub is rocking. Not only that, but unlike Melbourne it's open to the street, and the internal shenanigans are exposed for all to see. It's gay pride, it's safety in numbers, it's assumed acceptance. Music blares and only the roaring conversation from the packed house tops it. I head straight past the stage to what I assume is the dressing room door. I knock once and walk straight in to the glorified broom closet, stuffed to the roof with costumes and make-up. I'm confronted by two men in their late forties, both in a state of undress, with stocking caps and full drag make-up on. We blink at each other for a moment, and I introduce myself, saying that I'm playing Tick in the show. They instantly thaw, and with their pre-show hive of nervous energy enthusiastically shake my hand. I send Garry's apologies, and we swap small talk about how the show's going. Soon they usher me out so they can get ready for the show.

I prowl the pub for a good vantage point to see the stage. As I stand at the bar drinking my first beer, it becomes clear that I was flattering myself feeling nervous about standing here alone, since no one has even looked sideways at me. Either that or my gaydar is right off. I'm strangely miffed. I feel like I'm the only stranger at a roaring party of old friends.

Finally, the show begins. Music swells, and Cindy hits the tiny stage wearing a silver jumpsuit, and miming to a disco classic. No one even turns from their conversation to watch, and the chat level only rises to match the music. Cindy does everything to get their attention, but it's simply wallpaper to this heaving crowd.

I try to imagine how she's feeling. She's spotted me, and I can tell she's giving it everything for my benefit. She's an institution in the Sydney drag scene, but for all the effort she's gone to—making costumes with no money and choreographing intricate dance steps—she's nothing more than a colour and movement backdrop to the pulsing Thursday night crowd.

When she's finished she launches into shtick. She's surprisingly coarse and aggressive, perhaps to avenge the lack of attention from the crowd. She asks if there are any special celebrations in the crowd tonight. 'Not that I give a fuck,' she spits. A young woman down the front has brought her mum. Cindy takes one look at her and says, 'Oh, hello mother … fucker!' Drag queens seem to have the license to do or say whatever they like. Cindy gestures to me and says with a flourish, 'We've got a real life celebrity in the audience tonight.' I cringe slightly. 'Jeremy

Sandforth is here from the *Priscilla* show. You know how the film was based on my life story? Well Jeremy plays my character in the musical.' No one gives a shit, and they all turn back to their conversations.

Where in Melbourne Jess ruled the club with an iron fist, here in Sydney poor Cindy must turn somersaults to even score a passing glance. Sad but true, Cindy's misfortune tonight has been a gold mine of research for me.

On Friday morning, I climb the creaky wooden stairs to Anthony Phillip's Costumes once more. Like a concentration camp inmate, I strip to my undies in the cold as Anthony fits me with the now familiar corset. As he laces me in I tell him that the change into this corset is going to be very quick in the show. He rolls his eyes at Lizzy. Both of them are looking squeezed.

'How quick,' she asks through gritted teeth.

'About a minute,' I say.

She controls a moment of frustration.

'You'd think in a costume show like this we could have a bit more time to actually get into the *costumes*.'

'Wait till you see the Gumby change,' I say. 'I've got exactly twenty seconds for that one.'

She looks dumbly at me for a moment, checking I'm serious, and then she just walks away, shaking her head.

I'm much less self-conscious trying on my costumes today. I attract a crowd as I parade my vaguely mermaid-like 'Never Been To Me' outfit, which is nearly finished. Lizzy and Tim fuss over the waistline of my 'Shake Your Groove Thing' skirt. Tim fancies my legs and wants it to be as short as possible. For the first time in my life I'm being complimented on my shapely legs and cute arse. A guy could get used to this.

I take the opportunity to sneak a peek at the rest of the outfits that are finished. The funeral costumes hang in the warehouse looking incredible—like some bizarre

Beardsley Collection. I can't wait to see them on the dancers.

Ross is back. The Chita Rivera thing didn't go well. He did end up cancelling, but at late notice, and there's a lot of shit coming down on him because of it. A lot of people had bought very expensive tickets to see it and went away disgruntled. He didn't want to come back to Sydney at all, and now he's here he clearly wants to run away again. Out the front of the group today he's bereft of ideas, confidence and energy. He physically wilts in front of us.

Today's rehearsal is quite a picture though. Wardrobe had sent away to San Jose to buy up thirty pairs of stilettos big enough for the male ensemble to rehearse in. They've finally arrived, but the only colour they had was bright crimson. Subsequently, the entire ensemble, men and women, are all strapped into bright red stilettos and ready to dance. Tony struts in already wearing his. Coincidentally, he's worn a bright red shirt, which perfectly matches his shoes.

'Tony Sheldon! Look at your matching attire,' laughs Simon.

'You should see the purse,' Tony quips, without missing a beat.

4. The ensemble in their crimson stilettos.

We begin work on 'Colour My World', but it goes nowhere fast. Simon pushes Ross, trying to help him, but he has nothing left in the tank. His mood deteriorates, and the ensemble is left scratching their heads as they wait for something to do.

At one point a mobile phone rings. The room stops dead. This is a mortal sin because as well as drinks, bags and food, mobile phones are strictly outlawed in the rehearsal room. The usual penalty for a phone ringing in rehearsals is a slab of beer for the end of the week, but in a Simon Phillips rehearsal room the punishment is a bottle of Stolichnaya. I yell out that whoever owns the phone is up for this penalty.

Ross is forced to 'fess up that it's his phone, and without any sense of humour about it he snatches it up and turns it off. His phone has already rung a number of times in the rehearsals, and Simon teases him, trying to lighten his terrible mood.

'The problem with making Ross buy a punitive bottle of Stoli is that it doesn't represent a punishment to him at all,' Simon jokes.

Everyone laughs, but Ross looks daggers at Simon, marches over to the louvered windows, opens them, and drops his phone out onto the footpath four floors below. Everyone is speechless. Ross stomps back to his seat.

'There,' he says. 'It won't ring any more now, will it?'

By five o'clock everyone feels like we've gone through a grinder. The routine has been laborious, and we're all spent. Simon has to dash to Melbourne for MTC business, and as he leaves he jokingly instructs Ross to have something breathtaking for him to see on his return next week. The moment the door closes after him, Ross turns to us and says, 'What the fuck are we doing? We rush around catching planes, up here, down there, off to Melbourne, back up to Sydney. Into a cab, out of a cab, into a rehearsal room. We parade around in high heels learning these funny dance steps. It's madness.'

His monologue peters to a halt, his exhausted eyes begging us for a response. Everyone backs away politely, not quite knowing how to respond. He waves us away, calling a ten-minute break, and everyone eagerly scatters. I approach Ross, and I throw an arm around him as we walk out of the rehearsal room, but I don't have a clue what to say to him.

On the break, Tony has realised that I'm really not needed on Monday. I've been called for 2.00 pm, but it's only for my tiny appearance in 'Hot Stuff'. He marches into stage management to organise me a two-day weekend. I'm going home to Melbourne this weekend, so his efforts couldn't be more appreciated. He comes out looking triumphant and says, 'Sorted.' I could kiss him. I head to the airport for some desperately needed time with Annie and the kids.

Chapter 12
Rehearsals: Week 3

I kiss my sleeping boys and creep outside to the waiting cab, which toots selfishly in the freezing dawn. Half of me wants this madman's horn to wake them up so I can say a proper goodbye. It's been a frenzied weekend of children semi-attached to my limbs, odd jobs, quick, affectionate catch-ups in the schoolyard with friends as I deposit Hunter, and grasping at ways to describe to Annie what my last two weeks have entailed.

As I speed away toward my seven thirty flight, it all seems like a blur. I'm struggling to wake up, and I'm choking back tears from having to leave them behind again.

As I hit Sydney, I somehow reorganise my brain. I enter my other life. The lump in my throat dissolves and is replaced by a stirring of nerves in my stomach as I head through the 'crazy-maze' up to the rehearsal room.

Today is Tuesday, and we're working 'I Will Survive' with our Gumby shoes on. If the red stilettos were a rare sight to behold, these shoes take the biscuit. They're at least a metre long, thirty centimetres high, half a metre wide, and made of foam. You slip your foot into a sneaker, which is buried inside the foam. These things aren't easy to walk in, let alone dance in, and we begin the rehearsal struggling to even stand up. The entire ensemble staggers around in a state of shock, wondering whether this is an elaborate joke.

5. Struggling with our Gumby shoes.

Tony's face is stony. Not one to make a scene, he tends to absorb adversity, but he is clearly hating this. We struggle through the choreography like children learning to walk. It's jovial at first, but as it gets harder, and even painful, our collective good mood gutters. Tony later tells me that his bottom lip began quivering after a while as it was all too hard, and he just couldn't get the choreography. Jesus, did he take a look at me?

I have a lunchtime interview with a journalist at the

pub. My energy level is flatlining, and I'd much rather be relaxing. The journalist appears to be feeling the same way, so I work doubly hard to try and keep the interview swinging. Increasingly, journalists are being seduced by the 'fame' factor and seem to lose interest in a subject who isn't a film or pop star. This is certainly the case today. I'm clearly not on this journalist's radar, so I speak enthusiastically about the show and avoid talking about myself.

I dash back to work to find that we're going to run everything we've learnt so far. We start at the top and work our way through the entire show, putting it up on the floor. As each number comes around, I realise I can barely remember a thing. Some routines are a complete blank, and I only remember the choreography when I see others around me doing it. By the time we're finished I feel completely spent. As valuable as it was to re-cap, it's exposed just how far I've got to go.

While the ensemble work, 'Thank God I'm a Country Boy', the three queens run scenes with Simon. It's a huge relief as we've had little time dedicated to it. We run lines, revise blocking, and work on scenes we haven't put on their feet yet.

I love watching Simon stage scenes. He's got the whole picture in his head already. He tries to contrive moves with the actors that will fit with the rest of the big picture, but he still somehow remains true to keeping the actor at ease with the blocking.

Michael Caton joins us, and he approaches the work like a big kid, earnestly exploring his way through the scenes. He hasn't been on stage for many years, and he seems to be relishing his return.

On Thursday, the week seems to be speeding away from us. Most of the show is up on the floor, and we spend the day revising, setting quick-change timings, and finally choreographing 'MacArthur Park'.

Friday, and Spud has finished the "mega-mix". A show as camp as this could never do without one. Spud has made a medley of all the dance tracks from the show, and it will serve as the final, eye-popping climax and lead into the bows. Tim and Lizzy have designed an amazing collection of Australian flora and fauna costumes for the ensemble, and the number finishes with Tony, Dan, and I entering as the Sydney Opera House. It's going to look spectacular.

As the ensemble learns the voice parts for the mega-mix, Tony, Dan, and I are whisked away to choreograph 'Shake Your Groove Thing'. First we work the scene, and then Simon hands us over to Ross. He's been quiet and slumped all through the first part of the session, and he looks very brittle. Slowly, he draws himself up out of his chair and approaches us in silence, as though gathering himself. Absently, he asks where centre stage is. I point it out to him. The rehearsal room has never been so quiet. He wanders the stage in silence with a hand cupped over his chin, deep in thought.

'Play me the song?' he sighs.

Kath hits the tape deck, and we belt out the first few bars.

There's nothing more that I'd like to do
Than take the floor and dance with you,
Keep dancing, let's keep dancin'.

Ross snaps to and begins stepping through what could be the first few bars of the routine, but I instantly see a problem. The first lyrics are played as a moment for the three queens to steal themselves to go onstage. We lay our hands on top of each other, Three Musketeers-style, and lift them triumphantly. When the song starts properly we hit the stage, and that's when the routine should begin. I meekly interrupt Ross and point this out. He stops dead, looking like he's just been slapped. For a moment I think he's going to unleash on me, but this impulse falters, and instead he bursts into tears saying, 'I can't do this.' He runs out of the rehearsal room, Andrew chasing closely behind.

Time momentarily stops. Everyone is stunned. My heart sinks. In the vacuum that follows, I feel everyone's eyes on me. Simon is first to react.

'Jez, you know that wasn't about you.' Deep down I know this to be true—and there was always going to be one straw that would break this camel's back—but why did it have to be me? I feel dreadful for Ross. I want to chase him too, but it would be inappropriate and in the end not my duty today. He'll be in better hands with Andrew.

Simon calls a timely break. Gossip spills gravely about Ross' state of mind. I hear that he's been making late night calls to Garry, warning him how unhappy everyone is in the show, and saying that morale is at an all time low. This is just not true, and is clearly only Ross' bent perception of what is going on.

Tony says he was asked at a play he'd seen the night before if Ross had left the show. Apparently, this person had heard all kinds of rumours about Ross' difficulties.

Andrew appears hours later and takes me aside.

'Ross wants you to know that what happened had nothing to do with you.'

I ask how Ross is and he simply says, 'Not good,' and leaves it at that.

The grinding week finally turns to Saturday. As I arrive I'm informed that Ross is nowhere to be seen, and we'll be working through the show technically this morning. I'm not at all surprised, but I'm worried about when we'll actually see Ross again.

As I enter the rehearsal room, I hear Simon ask one of the ensemble cast how he's feeling. Apparently, he's been sick. I can hardly believe my ears. With all the madness going on around him, Simon still has the bandwidth to notice the intricacies of each personality in the cast.

Drama is coming at him from everywhere at the moment. Aside from the Ross dilemma, the music department is feeling the pressure of Simon changing things at will, and at times they have become resentful. The wardrobe department is behind schedule and flinch whenever Simon makes an adjustment. There's bound to be a fair whack of producer wrangling going on behind the scenes, too. Simon's still the artistic director of the MTC, and is constantly dealing with that business, but he takes on this high wire act with an amazingly thick skin and with incredible humour and good will, almost as if he thrives on it. Gradually, as things become more and more crazy, I see the cast turning to Simon with such love and respect, as a calming hand and a beacon of sanity.

6. Kath, Simon and Dean in rehearsals.

In the afternoon we do an entire run of the show. A posse of creatives has assembled to see how the show has taken shape and what their respective departments are in for. It's incredibly valuable for them, but I'm filled with dread. I don't feel ready to present this to anyone yet, even though these are 'friendlies'.

With my heart in my mouth we begin the run, and to my delight it goes surprisingly smoothly. The genuine rapturous applause at the end makes me think we're actually making a hit show. Some of the audience approach me afterwards, totally blown away at what good shape the show is in and how much they loved it. This is so encouraging, and I leave for the weekend feeling truly buoyed.

Trevor has organised a trip to The Imperial Hotel for me tonight to see the Priscilla drag show. It's been an institution at the pub for twelve years and is still going strong. He's very excited that I'm coming, and he meets me protectively at the door and escorts me over to a bunch of reserved tables in the corner. There seems to be no need for the reservation as the place is empty when I arrive at nine thirty.

'Don't worry, daaaaarrrrrling, it'll be packed by ten,' he sings.

Unlike the Newtown Hotel and its slick renovation, this pub has the atmosphere of an underground fringe theatre. The walls are painted and draped in black, and cigarette smoke hangs in the air. It reminds me of hidden clubs I used to go see bands in, back in the eighties.

There's a large stage at the far end, which looks like the focus of the club rather than the excuse for a stage at the Newtown. My wrist is stamped as I pay my cover charge, with ink so indelible that it will go to my grave with me.

The high priestess of this place is Mitzi Macintosh, perhaps the most high profile drag in Sydney. I find myself getting nervous flutters about meeting her. Trevor has promised an audience with her, and a trip backstage to see the costumes and the set up.

Priscilla cast members have begun to straggle in, all delighted and highly amused to see me here. They're also very protective of me. I'm guessing they may think I'll freak out with all these homosexuals around. The atmosphere pumps, and as Trevor predicted the room has filled up. He talks non-stop about the history of the place and about drag. Finally, it's time to go and meet Mitzi. I follow him through the magic doorway backstage, where a group of drags are flapping around applying monstrous amounts of make-up and cackling like banshees. Mitzi is already in drag and greets me regally, with the earned status of a celebrity. I'm slightly in awe in her presence, and she generously offers to show me around the catacomb that is backstage. She tour guides me up a staircase designed for elves, past racks and racks of dresses, all of them made or commissioned by her. One lit match would turn this place into an inferno. We climb to the next floor of the building and wander down the old style pub hallway, poking our noses into room after room filled with costumes.

Once these rooms housed nightly tenants on their way to somewhere else, or maybe those just too sozzled to get home. Now they drip with colourful outfits boasting years of work. I'm awed into silence. Mitzi must think me a shy little specimen.

We return to the gang, my mind still spinning at how devoted these people are to their work. The crowd crushes forward as the show begins, and I watch, now understanding that what I'm witnessing is not just a lifestyle, but a life.

Chapter 13
Rehearsals: Week 4

I can't believe we're into our fourth week of rehearsals. I can palpably feel the opening night approaching, but it still feels like there's a mountain to climb before we get there.

We assemble to finish 'Don't Leave Me This Way', which has been neglected in favour of so many other numbers. Ross grandly enters the rehearsal room, and everyone freezes, expectantly awaiting some kind of address from him, an apology, an explanation, but his absence isn't even touched on. It's like it never happened. I recognise his grandness is simply Ross being sheepish, too proud to expose himself before the gathered ensemble.

We begin the rehearsals, and to my horror Ross sinks into a ferocious mood. If anyone disappoints him or isn't quick to embody his choreography, he insults them. As the least adept dancer in the room I become terrified I'll be an easy target. This is not the Ross I know. I concentrate as best I can to avoid a swift verbal backhand from him. Amelia seems to cop more than her fair share, and I seek her out at the end of the session to make sure she hasn't taken it personally. She's straight out of drama school, and it would be easy for her to think she's disappointing her choreographer because she's just not up to it. This, of course, is not the case, she's an unbelievable talent, and I remind her of this and then explain that the Ross we're all experiencing at the moment is not his usual self, and he needs compassion despite his bad mood.

7. Dean Vince and I take a note from Ross.

Thankfully, at the end of the session, I'm no longer needed, so I go to the other studio to drill lines on my own. The ensemble has no choice but to endure a whole day of dodging Ross' volatile disposition. When they're finally released, I overhear one very experienced dancer describing today as the single worst day of his career.

Tuesday, and we return to 'Shake Your Groove Thing', the routine which inspired Ross' walk out last week. There's an unspoken unease in the room as we begin. I go out of my way to shut up. I exude compliance as I wait eagerly for my steps. But they don't come. Ross fidgets nervously as he waits for some kind of inspiration.

'I don't *do* steps,' he says, misting up. 'I just don't know what to do.'

We play the music over and over, and Ross finally begins setting the dance, one laborious step at a time. It takes forever.

Two hours pass, and we haven't even reached the halfway point of a two-minute routine. He apologises profusely as he tries to push through his terrible creative block. Simon is summoned to help but ends up just annoying him. Finally, Ross admits defeat and hands the routine over to Andrew. With Ross out of the room, Andrew finishes choreographing the routine in ten minutes.

The cast has bonded terrifically. Four groups have emerged for lunchtime activities. There's the park group, the café group, the stay at the rehearsal rooms group, and the pub group. I tend to float without loyalty. I love to observe the dynamics among a cast, because rehearsing a show is an incredibly intimate thing, and people become close. You tend to learn a lot about people very quickly. Today I get chatting to Damien about drag. He's one of the two drags in the show, and takes the whole lifestyle very seriously. He sees it as performance art, as well as a giant-sized hoot. He tells me being in drag liberates him, and he regularly goes out to clubs dressed as his drag character, Freeda Corsett.

'Oh, I'm a shocking bitch as Freeda,' he smirks. 'I can get anyone to do *anything* I want.' I look across at Trevor, who confirms this with a wry smile. 'All I have to do is snap my fingers,' he winks. He tells me this includes sexual favours, and he shares a few hair-raising stories of sexual conquests, mostly with so-called straight men, in bars, late at night.

'After they've struck out with the girls in the straight bars, they come to find *me*,' he pouts dryly.

His tales open the floodgates, and I'm swamped by other stories of conquests of straight guys from other members of the cast. It triggers a memory I have of a dresser I had once, telling me that the sexiest thing in the world was conquering a straight guy. I guess a lot goes on out there in the deep of the night.

David Page has left the show. I thought it was too good to be true that we had him in the first place. About two weeks ago he'd decided that ensemble work wasn't really his thing, and he'd departed. This left a huge hole in the show, because during the 'I Will Survive' number the three queens happen upon a group of indigenous people in the desert and end up dancing with them. It was crucial to have an Aboriginal performer for the scene. Replacing him has been an ongoing nightmare as the producers have found it hard to find an indigenous performer with the requisite musical theatre skills who wants to be in the show.

After a nervous two weeks they finally cast David's cousin, Kirk. He's a fine dancer and physical theatre performer, and he can sing beautifully. They've struck gold. It's Tuesday, and now Kirk's on board we can finally work on 'I Will Survive'.

We've choreographed the routine up until the Aboriginal people come into the song. That's when we've ground to a halt. Ross can now continue, but the big problem is that it's supposed to be a whole bunch of Aborigines, and we've only got one—and a few white chorus dancers. It's highly insulting to the indigenous community to have white people doing Aboriginal movement, and Kirk is quick to point this out. Generally, if white people want to use their movement, it must come with the indigenous community's permission. Kirk is now in the unenviable position of being asked to provide some movements, which our white cast can use with his blessing. But more than that, because Ross can't choreograph Kirk's movements either, it's going to be up to Kirk to choreograph himself. There's suddenly a tense standoff. Kirk states that he's not a choreographer, and that they should be getting in an indigenous choreographer to do the number, not relying on him. He's also worried about being appointed cultural ambassador and feels very awkward about it. Simon points out that they haven't the time or budget to bring anyone in, so the problem needs to be solved somehow.

This is all Ross needs. He's already fragile, and I can see him trying hard to respect Kirk's cultural sensitivities, but his frustration is at melting point. He makes a start, trying to give Kirk some movements, but everything he tries either offends Kirk, or Ross hates it.

The ensemble sits around waiting to be plugged into the session, alive to the terrible tension in the room. With nothing to do, Simon takes Tony, Dan, and me away to run scenes. Part of me wants to stay to see how the process unfolds, but I'm mostly relieved to be leaving the pressure cooker behind.

After an hour or so, we're ready to return to the choreography room. We're all desperate to know how they've gone on. As we troupe back in, a gaggle of producers arrive for a six o'clock meeting, opting to come early so they can see some rehearsals in action. Simon's face falls.

'Why, why, why?' he mumbles, 'of all the sessions to come and see, did they choose this one?' We all know this could be a monumental failure.

As we haven't been put into the dance yet, Tony, Dan, and I sit with the producers to watch the routine with Andrew and Dean filling in for our parts. Simon is twitchy. He likes to be across everything, and right now he's in the dark, like everyone else. We wait nervously as the dancers take their place. The producers are eager to watch, and completely unaware of the preceding drama.

Are we all about to witness a car crash?

The music rolls and the dance starts. Kirk leaps around the stage doing an amazing series of cartwheels and indigenous style dance moves. It has an instant dramatic impact and is thrilling to watch. It's like nothing we've seen so far in the show.

The white 'indigenous' people have been buried up the back, and their movement is simple and non-specific. When it finishes there's a shriek from the onlookers. I look across at the producers and their faces are lit up with smiles. Simon breathes a sigh of relief. This is a huge victory for Ross, both creatively and personally.

It's Thursday, and after a morning of re-capping and an interview at lunchtime, I'm introduced to the boys who are playing my son. There are four of them, and they'll play the role on a rotational basis. They're all aged nine and seem like a bunch of bright sparks. I burn their names into my memory so I don't embarrass myself by calling them by the wrong name. They know their lines and seem to have been drilled in great detail. We play the scenes through, giving each one a shot at it, and they do exceptionally well.

On Friday we have a run of the show. It sends jitters through everyone. I overhear members of the ensemble muttering about how they can't remember anything. This is outrageous, as every time I see them doing anything they seem incredibly well drilled.

Tony informs me that *The 7.30 Report* will be filming it as part of a story they're doing on the show. I can't believe we haven't been told about this. Communication isn't a strong point from out of the citadel.

I make a pact with myself to throw everything at this run to see how far I've come. In all the runs I've done so far, I've kept something back, testing how things play, choosing not to commit to some moments until I've truly worked them out. This is the opposite of how Tony works. He goes in boots and all, bravely playing everything to the hilt with no fear of failure. I'm in awe of his courage and have decided to adopt the Sheldon approach for today.

The run goes incredibly well, particularly for the ensemble. It's starting to look like a show. We're really getting the feel of how it will work dynamically, and it seems to have a fabulous flow.

Afterwards, Simon calls the principals together for a quick debrief. I'm worried. Perhaps we're about to get the 'C'mon, lads, it's two weeks until previews, let's lift our game,' speech. Instead of a towelling, Simon seems very happy and asks *us* if we have any concerns we need to talk about. None of us do, aside from the appropriate state of panic we're all in.

I pack my bags for Melbourne this morning. I'm going straight to the airport after work to spend the weekend at home. I'm just hanging on. The kids have got bored with having to talk to me on the phone, so I get little communication with them beyond, 'Hi, Dad and bye, Dad.' I'm aching to spend some time with them.

In the afternoon, the boys playing Benji, my son, are back in. We're going to set the staging for 'Say A Little Prayer'. Benji appears in my imagination, and I sing the song to him.

I sing it through a few times so Simon can get a grip on when Benji should appear and where he should move on stage. We try it a few ways, with varying success. The best version we find has him walking past me, suddenly catching my attention. I watch him as he runs to Marion, my wife, and they walk away together.

We have to play the scene through with each boy so they can all learn it, but after about the third time through I start to get misty. Watching the Benji character walk away from me reminds me of my own sons being so far away, and I can't stop feeling achingly homesick. By the fourth run, I burst into tears. I'm in the middle of the song, and I begin to sob uncontrollably. The rehearsal stops, and everyone turns to me, bewildered. After a moment of shock, Simon asks, 'Are you okay?'

This is exactly the wrong question.

'I just miss my boys so much,' I sob, and then completely lose it. I'm simultaneously embarrassed about crying in front of the kids *and* the cast, and desperate to pull myself together so I can continue the rehearsal. But I can't. Tears stream down my face, and I leave the room to gather myself. I stand in the windy corridor trying to avoid the passing foot traffic. A cheerful company manager waves at me as she passes. Her face drops when she sees my soaking face.

'Are you okay?' she pleads.

'I'm fine,' I lie, and insist she leave me alone.

After a few sooky minutes, I return to the room to continue work. I apologise and assure everyone I'm fine now. Marney approaches and gives me a hug. As sweet as it is, I have to push her away in case I start all over again.

We run the scene and that's exactly what happens. I feel so brittle and tears are so close to the surface that once the song starts, so do the tears. I'm furious with myself. I feel so stupid that I can't work the scene. I draw together all my will power and start once more. This time it works. With a sense of relief, Simon finally finishes staging the scene, and we're all free to go home. I make my dash to the airport. I can't wait to see my real boys.

Chapter 14
Rehearsals: Week 5

To avoid the mad dash in the morning, I get a plane back from Melbourne on Monday night. The weekend went past in a blur, and the closer I get to Sydney the more it hits me that the comfortable buffer zone between being in the rehearsal room and being on stage on the opening night is about to be taken away. It's Tuesday, our last day at Brent Street.

I begin the day with a photo shoot at the theatre. Never having done a show in the Sydney Lyric theatre before, it feels unfamiliar and somehow imposing. I can't yet navigate the corridors, and like most new theatres it lacks any wholesome, old-style atmosphere. The large, echoing corridors are built for practicality, not beauty, and in an attempt to actually present as a theatre, a host of framed posters boasting the slate of shows previously performed here self-consciously line the corridors.

Once I sign in at stage door, I take the lift up to the green room to meet Tim, who will be in the photo with me.

'Hi, sexy,' he purrs, and he slips me into my emerald 'I've Never Been To Me' outfit. This is my first publicity call in drag, and I have more than a few butterflies wondering how this shot is going to turn out. It'll be printed in colour in The Weekend Australian Magazine, and plenty of people are going to catch an eyeful of it.

The photographer is disorganised and indecisive. On top of that, she doesn't know or particularly care who Tim is. She orders him around like he's my dresser. I introduce him to her again, pointedly reminding her that he's one of the designers of the show, but she seems to care little. Tim isn't worried and seems more nervous about being in the photo than offended by her manner.

She suggests we go outside for the shot, and ushers me to the courtyard outside the green room. It's raining. It's also grimy on the tiles, and my emerald mermaid-like outfit has a tulle train, which drapes along the ground. I point out that the dress may be damaged. She screws up her face like a spoilt valley girl and tries to assure me it'll be okay. I refuse to go outside in the rain, and she reluctantly moves the shot inside. She decides she needs more light and rushes out to her car to get some equipment. This takes her fifteen minutes, and when she finally returns she begins to assemble an impressive rig of lights. She apologises profusely, but Tim and I are getting less and less patient with her.

Finally, she's ready and we snap some shots. She turns the camera around and shows me what she's taken. It was certainly worth the wait. The shots look fabulous, and the lighting is terrific. The dress comes up beautifully in all its emerald splendour. I feel enormously relieved that I'm going to pull off my drag debut in style.

Now late, I race back to Brent Street for our final day of rehearsal. The cast has been finishing off the mega-mix choreography. Tony, Dan, and I only enter at the end of the routine, dressed as the Sydney Opera House, so we wait outside the room until they've finished. Finally, we're called in to watch a run of it. Ross is brimming with pride as we take our seats.

The music starts and the routine begins. It's amazing. To imagine all the colours and the costumes parading around in this dazzling routine is really exciting. I look across at Tony, and tears of pride are running down his face. This is the man who argued against having a mega-mix in the first place. Watching him in tears, I feel absolved for *my* sookiness on Saturday.

In the afternoon we do a final run of the show. This is such an important run, being the last we'll do until dress rehearsal. All the producers and designers will be there, eager to see how far we've come.

The run goes incredibly well. Everyone steps it up a gear, particularly Tony. I feel like each time he steps up a gear he puts Dan and me on notice to follow suit—keep working hard or get lost in his dust.

I feel very proud of Ross. It's been a nightmare for him, and as much as he's put a lot of people through hell to get there, he's definitely come up with the goods. The choreography looks fabulous, and when everything calms down and we've put all the drama behind us, we'll be left with his wonderful work.

I wind my way through the labyrinth to the outside world for the last time. I'm so glad to be out of that filthy, cold, windy, pigeon-infested hole. Tomorrow we move into the theatre, and the real magic begins.

I begin Wednesday with a costume fitting. Anthony is really showing the strain today. He works quickly and tugs at my corset just that little bit too roughly, as if his mind is on a million other things. I try to draw him on how things are going, but he remains tight lipped and professional, only offering that things are a little stretched. The lead up to previews will be gargantuan. My outfits are nearly finished and look truly amazing.

When I get to the theatre there's a siren blaring. The cast, crew, and staff are pouring out the stage door for a fire drill. This is modern theatre. Everyone has to be inducted—shown the safety procedures and the alarms. Don't worry about the hundreds of people up and down the promenade by the casino who'll think the place is burning down.

Once upon a time when you went to a theatre, there'd be a stage door man to greet you politely and wish you well for the show as you signed on. In new theatres it's become like Fort Knox, with security guards and passes and swipe cards.

I head to the stage, which has already been painted a deep rusty red. It's a cavernous space, and the red seems to enhance its size. I pause for a moment and look out to the auditorium, currently a mass of empty seats. I try to imagine them filled and me on stage, performing this show to them. The thought gives me a flutter.

Kath arrives and shows me to my dressing room, which is stark. It has a couch, a dressing table and mirror, surrounded by lights, and a separate shower and toilet, like a compressed hotel room. Each performer in a long run quickly decorates their room with their own particular flair. I can already see where my children's pictures will hang.

This morning is my favourite part of any production period: the Sitzprobe. The band and the cast are assembled, and will play through the songs together for the first time. After rehearsing to either piano or backing tracks, we finally get to hear how the arrangements sound in all their glory.

We're called onto the huge stage, where a long line of chairs have been assembled, facing out to the auditorium. Four mics have been set up on stands for the singers to gather round when it's their turn to sing. As we take our seats, I see Spud prowling the auditorium, geeing up the band. He plays it cool, but I can tell he's excited.

Once we're seated, he introduces the band, saying that these guys are the best of the best. To give us the proof, he chooses the most impressive number to begin with, 'MacArthur Park'. He says he wants us to hear the arrangement first before we sing it, and he strikes up the band. They play the number through and, as promised, it's enormous. It sweeps us all away. By the end, everyone's cheering. Then we play through it again, but this time we sing along. It sounds doubly amazing with the vocals.

Then we begin at the top of the show and work our way through. Each number has its own little surprise and is a thrill to hear. We get to 'Always On My Mind', and I get a rush of nerves as I approach the mic to sing. The arrangement sounds beautiful, and I do my best to sing it as well as I can. When I finish I turn to go back to my seat and notice all the girls, (male *and* female) are in tears.

We sing through 'Pop Muzik'. When we finish, Spud comes up on stage to ask why the ensemble is singing a certain vocal part that wasn't in the arrangement. One of them says Ross wanted it sung to go with a certain piece of choreography. Spud curls his lip and quips, 'I've got some choreography I'd like to try out later too.'

At lunchtime, Dan, Tony, and I get into drag make-up and costume for an interview with Deborah Hutton. There's been a ridiculously short time allocated to getting ready. There are only two make-up artists for three of us, and we only have an hour. Add to that we're being filmed by a TV crew who insist on turning off the dressing table lights because they interfere with the camera. Cassie and her assistant, Ben, work like fury. At 2.00 pm we're due on stage, but we're not nearly ready and my shoes and corset have gone missing. Carl rushes in insisting that we're due on stage *right now*. Cassie rolls her eyes as if to say, 'We'll be there when we're there!'

It's the first time since the auditions that I've been in drag make-up. This time the make-up is much better, and with the flowing blonde wig I look incredibly glamorous—and strangely like Jessica Rabbit. My last appearance in drag had an agenda of ambition attached to it, so this time, without having to prove anything, and with the confidence of feeling far more attractive, something inside me feels ready to be unleashed.

I head to the stage and find the ensemble sitting in the auditorium having some down time. Unable to believe their eyes, they absolutely scream when they see my transformation. The outfit completely takes me over, and I strut down to the front of stage and start spitting bitchy comments out.

'If things don't get moving on this call, I'll be going back to my fucking trailer!' I snap. The cast fall about laughing, and it only adds fuel to the fire. 'Like my tits?' I purr. 'At least they're real, unlike *some* people's.' I turn and gesture to Deborah, who eyes me uneasily. 'I cannot *beeeleeeeve* I've come looking more glamorous than Deborah Hutton, poor little thing.' The cast are in stitches, and I have to be physically dragged off to do the interview with Deborah.

Freeda warned me that being in drag gives you the license to do or say whatever you want. Well, here's the proof. I've become a bitchy, prima donna, spouting spite like some faded movie Goddess. I feel liberated, like I can be forgiven for saying whatever the hell I want. Everyone knows it's an act, everyone knows it's just little old me under this garb, but that makes it all the funnier. It's the classic actor's tool. Provide a funny hat, or a mask, or a walking cane and you're someone completely different. The costume takes you over. The place this outfit has taken me to is squarely into being a drag queen: a singularly unique persona. I'm not, as Amanda Munroe would have me believe, giving the straight guys a secret erection. I'm not pushing any boundaries of my own sexuality; I'm simply being a drag queen—the natural response to dressing up as a glamorous woman and playing her to the hilt. As an actor, I'm doing what I do, which is playing a role.

8. Jessica Rabbit.

Years ago I played in a glam rock cover band called the Melody Lords. We covered all the biggies like Gary Glitter, The Sweet and Suzi Quatro. It was comedy and rock 'n 'roll, and for a time we were the biggest cover band in Melbourne. Glam is a kind of macho, music hall version of drag. It's a rock 'n' roll, dress-up fantasy in a 'call me a poof, and I'll kick your head in' sort of a way. We dressed in wigs and make-up in the glam style, and each member of the band adopted the clownish archetype of a 70s rocker. I was the sex kitten, Throbbing Glitteris, who sported a long, curly Peter Frampton hairstyle, Red Symons' Skyhooks make-up, and who pretended to fuck anything that had a pulse. Throbbing used to set me free in the same way this outfit is now. Between songs I could hit the microphone and spout the most outrageous tales of groupies and sex and debauchery. All of it lies, all of it made up on the spot but funny because it came from inside that character, that wig and that make-up.

I do the interview with Deborah. She's cautious throughout. We've never met with me dressed as a male, so the 'me' she's dealing with is a frightening creature. I find I simply can't let my drag character drop. I pose and pout and vainly admire myself in any reflecting surface the entire time.

Deborah, I can tell, can't wait to escape the monster, and when it's finally over she makes a dash for it. We scrub off the caked inches of make-up and head back to the stage for mic checks. I dissolve back to little old me again. I'm approached over and over by members of the ensemble, still reeling with the transition, which overtook me. I feel like I've just sobered up from a particularly heavy night of drinking and am being reminded of what I did.

We spend the afternoon having our head mics fitted and tested. The sound department gets levels as we chat through our dialogue. Boy, it's been a very long day.

After a restless night's sleep, I make my way to the theatre for more sound checking. I feel churned today, nervous. I ask Tony how he's feeling, and he says he was nervous all day yesterday.

Dan is in the dressing room next door to me. He has totally moved in. He's turned it into his private lounge room. He's brought in prints and a sound system and draped his couch in beautiful fabric. He's even talking about buying a bar fridge. My dressing room seems very stark by contrast.

Today we space the choreography. We're being placed exactly where we should be on the stage. It's time consuming and is crucial to avoid anyone running into sets or other dancers. Much to Spud and Ross' frustration, people come in and out of rehearsal, as they are whisked away for costume fittings.

It's Friday, and the ensemble are away at a recording studio putting down vocals for the click track. Because this show is so physical to perform, the live vocals will be helped along by a recorded version, which will play along with the show. It's cheating, but no one will ever know.

This gives the principles some time on stage to work the scenes with Simon. It's such a luxury, and being on stage liberates my performance. Trying to perform in a rehearsal room is stuffy because you always have the director staring you in the face. I feel self-conscious most of the time, but now I feel a sense of ease about it, and the scenes work well.

Yesterday, Simon had given us rewrites of about five scenes. We learnt them overnight, and we try them out now.

At lunch, Garry approaches me about a possible publicity call for next Friday. It's a nightmare because it means cancelling some of our technical rehearsal time to do it, but he justifies it by saying it's a huge publicity coup. It will be at a very big, 'high society' fundraiser, which will be attended by the Prime Minister. My face drops.

'Do you have a problem with that?' he asks.

'I do,' I tell him, quickly thinking through how to handle this. I'm by no means a Prime Minister John Howard lover, and I have no desire to be in the same room with him.

'I'll do it,' I say, 'but only if I don't have to meet him. If I had to meet him, I'd be rude to him and that would reflect badly on the show.'

Garry is a little bewildered, but cops it. He agrees and says if we do it he'll make sure I'm not put in that position.

Saturday sees us working with the revolve. Simon and the stage crew have been here practically all night, timing how things will appear on it. Each specific cue must be timed to the second, or important entrances of props, set, or performers will not work. It takes most of the day and brings us to the end of our last week of proper rehearsals. Next week is tech week, and I can feel everyone gearing up for it. I've already braced myself, knowing that in this show it will be the mother of all tech weeks. Heaven help us.

Chapter 15

Bustration

Tech week

Worlds collide. Today I extract my excited family from the airport and absorb them into my Sydney bachelor life. I realise that although I've been missing them like hell, the pain of their absence has slowly ebbed away in the time I've been here. The heart truly is an adaptable muscle.

I can hear the boys' excited chat as they bounce up the aerobridge to the gate lounge. When they spot me in the crowd they run into my arms like a Myer's ad for Father's Day. The picture is complete. There's an irreplaceable joy when a family is together. They take turns with piggyback rides on the way to the car park, and I bask in the unbridled love the boys shower on me.

We play games in the car, trying to guess which apartment block is our new home in Sydney as we approach the Medina. Their excitement level spins out of control as we pass our very own pool on our way to the room. The boys choose their beds, and we unpack the suitcases like we're on holiday. Annie is thrilled at the prospect of a serviced apartment, and a husband to throw some weight around two increasingly rebellious boys.

This is a two-day weekend for me as we're now on a Tuesday to Sunday working week. It passes like we're on holiday, with trips to the beach, the pool and the local playgrounds. The kids only stop chattering when they're asleep.

As Tuesday morning approaches, I begin to suck up all my reserves of fortitude. I know this is going to be huge. Thankfully, Annie knows all about technical rehearsals, so when I sheepishly bid farewell to her on Tuesday morning and say I'll see her next Monday, she understands exactly what I mean.

Let me define technical rehearsals. As actors, we've already rehearsed how the show goes. Now, as we put it into the theatre, every technical aspect of the show must be put into place. The lighting, the costumes, the sound, the sets—all must fit seamlessly around the scenes. Each technical department creates a recipe for how to put the show on. Lights have to go up at the right times, sound has to be at the right level and so on. All these things become cues, called by the stage manager as the show is performed. It's a grindingly slow process and deeply frustrating. Because this show is so highly technical I've braced myself for the worst. I'm guessing it will be about four times worse than the next worst show I've had to tech, which was *Hello, Dolly!* We teched that for three straight days before we even got up to the end of the first number. But *Hello, Dolly!* was a show that had been done before. *Priscilla* is a brand new piece, and there is no recipe for how it should be done. No one knows what will work and what won't.

I arrive at the theatre to meet my dresser, Troy, who seems to have a shallow but calm grasp on what is happening. His plot for me is vague, and we can't work out which outfit I should start the show in. With everyone in authority madly attending to a million other things, we take a stab at what I should wear from the huge pile of costumes filling my dressing room.

We're called onto the stage. Simon addresses us, warning us about the hell we have ahead. He says there are lots of things that aren't ready or haven't arrived yet: sets, costumes, props. He asks us to please be patient.

The scene backstage resembles an ants' nest that has been poked with a stick. The stage management team, whose job it is to keep order, is doing its best to reign in the anarchy via constant messages over their headsets, and announcements through the Tannoy (the theatre speaker system), but the bustling workers scatter in all directions, attempting to get their specific piece of the impossible workload done before the rehearsal kicks off.

I'm waiting in my dressing room, wearing the wrong costume. It's only because Anthony rushes past and sees me and quickly plucks out the right one that I start the day in the correct one.

We begin with 'Downtown'. First up, the Divas fly in from the roof and sing the number suspended high above the stage. The timing of this must be done to coincide with a music cue, and it takes a few goes to get it right. The girls are still getting used to the feeling of hanging so high in the air. Now they're being asked to sing and perform their choreography at the same time. It's a huge ask, and I get the feeling they're only just managing.

Once that's plotted, the ensemble begins their dance. Lights are focused on specific places on stage as they run the routine, and then I enter. Once I'm on stage, the revolve brings on the dressing room lights. I'm supposed to get changed in front of them for 'I've Never Been To Me', but the revolve doesn't work. The song grinds to a stop. We begin at the start and try again. We get up to the moment the revolve should start, and it breaks down again. There are many frustrated sighs and much scratching of heads, until someone realises that the jostling of the dancers feet on the revolve has confused the computer that drives it and has made it crash. Until the program can be re-written to tell the computer not to do that, the dancers are instructed to keep off the revolve until it starts its cue.

We get up to my quick change into 'I've Never Been To Me'. I have a specific amount of bars to get out of my costume and into my green dress before I have to exit and then come on to do the number. We run it, and of course I'm nowhere near making it. Part of the problem is the high heels I've been given. They haven't been designed for a quick change. I can't for the life of me understand why I've ended up with shoes that are so hard to do up. Someone rushes up to demonstrate how easy they are to get on. They fail. We try again and again. I'm constantly assured it will get easier, but it's crystal clear to me that the design is just wrong. I pull my first prima donna moment of the day and flatly say I want new shoes. Without blinking they oblige. There will be new shoes. I'm greatly relieved.

On the break, the make-up masks arrive. It's the first time I've clapped eyes on them. The Devo guys have certainly come through with the goods. They're an amazing innovation. About the size of a large pair of sunglasses, they fit exactly onto your face and have the drag make-up already painted on them. They also have false eyelashes attached. I slip one on, and I'm instantly a drag queen. What the girls at the Imperial wouldn't do for a set of these.

We go into 'I've Never Been To Me', and I enter the stage with my mask, wig and emerald dress on. It feels very strange being so swathed in attire, almost like I can't be seen underneath it all. As I do the number I'm slowly pushed onto stage on a moving platform. I struggle to keep my balance in my high heels as I mime. It's quite terrifying. I get through it, and I exit for my next change, which I know we won't get to for ages. Ross barrels up to me gasping about how brilliant the mask looks. He says that from the audience it's impossible to tell it's a mask.

Backstage, it's become commonplace to see performers wandering around in corsets, bizarre wigs, or wearing little more than stockings. It hardly raises an eyebrow. The crew are too busy to notice and are constantly sighing with frustration that a piece of set hasn't arrived yet, so they can't test how it will fly in. Strictly speaking, this makes the tech run pointless because absolutely everything should be right before we move on. But without all the ingredients at our disposal we simply have no choice.

The rest of the day is spent timing entries and exits on the revolve. Time flies past, and by the end of the day we've teched about ten minutes of the show. Not a bad outcome really. Troy can write up what my first two outfits are, and tomorrow we'll take a guess at what my next one will be.

On Wednesday we arrive early to start on the choreography for the John Howard, Luna Park gig. It means changing the Gumby dance to accommodate a different stage. I've still only got a limited grasp on the actual choreography, so I find it a complete mind-fuck to alter it. There's little enthusiasm for the call as all our heads are in the tech of the show, and this is just an annoying distraction.

When we finish, a company meeting is called. Sandra, our company manager, begins to outline all the extra-curricular work they're about to put us through. As well as the Luna Park gig, the ensemble has a film shoot tomorrow for the video footage which is screened in *Hot Stuff*, we have a big press call on Tuesday, as well as pictures for the program and a film shoot for the TV ad. A collective groan fills the room. Everyone is painfully aware how slowly the tech has been moving so far, and murmurs are beginning to spread amongst the cast that we won't be ready for our first preview next Wednesday.

Now with all these other distractions thrown in it's hard to fathom how we can possibly get it all done. Dan pipes up and asks what happens if we aren't ready for the first preview. Without blinking or a flicker of doubt, Sandra shoots back, 'We just will be.'

The tech rehearsal picks up where we left it yesterday. Before long we arrive at the much-anticipated entrance of the bus. This is the most impressive piece of set I've ever seen. It really, *really* looks like a bus, and it has so many functions it's mind blowing. I try to put a price tag on it as I see it floating across the stage for the first time. It must be worth a million dollars. It's equipped with GPS navigation so the computer that drives it knows exactly where it is on stage down to the last millimetre. Because, like everything else on this show, it has arrived a week late, the tech heads haven't had any time to try it out. Put simply, they don't know how to work it. The program that's supposed to tell it where to go on stage, the path to take to get it there, and how long it has to do it, has not been written yet. Therefore, every time the bus moves, the programmers have to write a complete plot for the bus and load it into the computer.

At the beginning of 'Go West' the bus enters for the first time. It sweeps downstage and does a three hundred and sixty degree turn and then stops, at which point the three queens board it and it turns one hundred and eighty degrees. Then the side opens up so the audience can see us performing the next scene. All of this has to happen in an exact amount of time because it's all set to music. We play the scene over and over as the timing of the bus is explored. With each failure, the bus has to be reset to start over. Each pass at it takes about half an hour to organise, and it's grindingly slow and frustrating. Nearly the entire day is spent on this one particular movement. I scan through the show, trying to approximate how many of these kinds of movements the bus does, and I come up with dozens. If you do the math, there's no way we will get through teching the bus alone before next week. To make matters worse, the bus has safety sensors at the front and rear, which if touched, shut the bus down immediately. We've discovered that if something is placed on the revolve and the bus hits it, it will stop. We then have to spend half an hour resetting so as to work out how *not* to hit the bus with that particular piece of set.

At one stage, amongst all this angst, I find myself relaxing inside the bus as it's reset for the millionth time. Inside, it's dressed like the inside of some luscious genie bottle. As it rotates, the world seems to turn all around me. Coloured lights dance on the fancy bus dressing, and I lose all perspective of which way I'm facing. I have a moment of clarity. I'm suddenly acutely aware of how fortunate I am to be part of this thing, this huge beast of a show. So many people would have given anything to be sitting where I am right now.

'Aren't we lucky,' I say out loud to my fellow travellers, Tony and Dan. Dan thinks I'm being sarcastic.

'Yeah,' he says, rolling his eyes.

'No, really,' I say. 'This is truly amazing. We're so lucky.'

On a break I'm fitted with another shirt. Simon has already scrapped the costume for the first bus trip. He apparently hated the shirt under the lights and asked for another. The wardrobe department raced away to find what else they could come up with, and this is it. I slip it on with the knowledge that this one too may be scrapped in the coming days.

It's Thursday morning and the cast are all in Paddington, shooting the vision for *Hot Stuff*. Tony and I have a press call and have to get into full drag make-up once more. Dare I say it: this is becoming run of the mill.

After an hour and a half of make-up we head to the stage and shake it for the camera. This is for a front page spread in the Daily Telegraph, so it has to look good. It's the first time the bus has been photographed too, and the producers are keen to get lots of it in the shot. To the uninitiated, it will look disappointing because it looks so much like a real bus. It's only when you see it in context and realise what the thing can actually do that it blows you away.

We get out of make-up for the afternoon's tech. An hour and a half to put it on, five minutes to wash it off—it seems such a waste.

All the cast is assembled in the rehearsal room for a company meeting. This time we know it's big because Garry is present. Tony leans across to me and whispers, 'What's the bet they've cancelled the first preview?'

As Garry goes to speak you could hear a pin drop. Everything at this stage of a production seems vulnerable. So much can go wrong. This announcement could as easily be about more publicity as it could be about cancelling previews.

Garry starts.

'As you're painfully aware, a lot of stuff isn't ready in this show yet. Simon and I are feeling a bit like we're not actually teching *anything* properly because we're missing so much of the show. As a result we've decided to give the stage over to the techies for forty-eight hours so they can finish getting the stage ready, and then we'll start teching again on Saturday from the beginning of the show with everything in place. Also, we've decided to cancel the Wednesday and Thursday previews. Our first public show, which we can't cancel because it is a sold out charity event for the AIDS Council of New South Wales, will be Friday night.'

There's a stunned silence as everyone takes this in. The previews being cancelled seemed inevitable, but what do we *do* in the meantime while the stage isn't free?

Simon says we'll work through choreography, scenes, and songs while we wait. He also wants to see a costume parade by the principles. And this is exactly what happens.

One minute I'm singing, next I'm dancing. Finally, I finish the day parading all my finished costumes for Simon, Tim, Lizzy, and Anthony. Simon makes adjustments, changes colours for some, and throws some things out. Amazingly, the wardrobe department defer to him, agreeing to everything he asks for.

Friday arrives, which means we're assembled with military precision to board the Priscilla bus, and we're herded off to Luna Park to rehearse for our big gig in front of the Prime Minister.

We pack onto the bus. I feel like I'm in a music video as we roar across the Sydney Harbour Bridge in the brilliant sunshine. The excitement level is intense, and we all behave like a bunch of naughty school kids let loose on an unsuspecting world.

The function centre at Luna Park has its best frock on for the night, and all the ornately laid out tables face inwards to the stage where we, amongst others, will strut our stuff tonight. We work our number in civvies, until all the technical staff are across it, and then we change into our outrageous Gumby costumes. Our headpieces and shoes are so enormous it's an almost impossible task to dance in them. The unsuspecting crew at the event gape as we return frocked up.

Once we're drilled, we return to the bus and are shipped back to the theatre to continue doing anything that might make opening night not seem so improbable.

On my return, I'm introduced to Zoë, a beautician from the casino's beauty parlour, who sports the perky good looks you'd expect from someone in her position. She has a well-groomed authority now, but it's very easy to get a sniff of the wild child she'll become the moment she knocks off at six.

Sandra suggests we make a time for me to get waxed. I gulp and ask if this is really necessary. Apparently, it's crucial. Without really thinking it through, I find myself spilling the fact that I have two hours off right now.

Zoë grins. 'Then we'll do it now.'

I'm completely snookered. My head spins with exit strategies, but sensing my unease Zoë takes control. She flicks me a sassy smile. 'Come on,' she purrs, 'I'll be gentle.' She takes my hand and leads me away from the terribly amused Sandra.

She escorts me politely through the casino and up to the lavish salon on the eighth floor, where rich Japanese businessmen's wives are talked through the salon's menu of services in their own language. She shows me into a small, climate controlled room with a spectacular view of the harbour, and asks me to strip off.

'Everything?' I squeak.

'Everything,' she says flatly, and vacates the room as a feeble nod to my privacy. When I'm finally lying naked, face up on the bed, my modesty covered by only the tiniest cut of terry towelling, she returns with the appropriate implements. I chat nervously, like I'm about to get a vasectomy.

'How much of me will you do?'

'Everything,' she says matter of factly. And then undoes her cool authority with a cheeky wink. 'Except your bits.' I breathe a sigh of relief.

'This your first time?' she asks, like a nurse distracting me before an injection.

'Yep.'

'It's not so bad. And I'm the *best*.' She puts all the innuendo of a *Carry On* movie into her delivery of the word best, and then she begins.

She gently parts my legs and spreads the first swipe of warm wax right up my inner thigh. It sends tingles straight to my groin, and I read in her expression that she's slightly pleased with herself, like she knew it would. She makes another pass, lingering, just so, at the top of it. It's completely erotic, and some serious embarrassment will soon follow if this keeps up. She takes a long strip of fabric from a pile on the bench and lays it across my warm thigh. She presses on the cloth gently but firmly with her fingertips.

'Deep breath,' she says, and then without warning, tears it from my skin. I erupt with surprise more than pain. My leg feels like it's been spanked, and the prickling tingle which follows the warmth of the wax is the perfect partner for what could only be described as a kind of wild, erotic foreplay. Bewildered, I look up at her. She's beaming like she's just taken my virginity.

'I'm *loving* my job right now,' she croons, and lays the fabric a second time. She rips it and pouts knowingly at me.

Then she goes back for her little spatula, dripping the gooey, pink wax once more. With it, she heads further north into my groin, casually readjusting my genitals out of the way as she goes. The uninhibited way in which she tosses them around makes me feel as though I should be completely at ease with it, but the only person to handle me with such nonchalance for many, many years has been my dear wife. I begin to question if this is a regular visit to the waxing lounge, or whether I'm getting any special attention. She rips the fabric off again, and this time it stings a great deal more. I yelp.

'Yep,' she says, 'That's gonna hurt. Sorry, honey.' And then she repeats, 'I am *soooo* loving my job right now.'

I spend the session desperately fighting off arousal and talking quickly over my nervousness.

As promised, she waxes everything but 'my bits', and I go to the shower feeling like one of those strange, hairless cats—one that's been plunged into a tub of water.

Zoë waves me goodbye with the satisfied look of a woman who has just had a weekend of the best sex of her life. I totter to the lift feeling light-headed with confusion. My legs feel bizarre beneath my jeans. The moment I arrive back to the theatre I am plonked into the make-up chair to get into drag for tonight's gig. This really is a strange job.

At 8.45 pm we leave for Luna Park. This time we travel in a limo. A broadcast of an AFL footy final is on the radio. I become conscious that I'm vigorously cheering on the Sydney Swans whilst sitting in full drag make-up in the back seat. While I cheer, I'm vaguely aware that I'm taking care not to smudge my lipstick. Not a picture of your classic footy fanatic.

The venue is teeming with security, and we have to pass a number of checkpoints to get in. We're taken upstairs to the green room, where we bump into the other performers and celebrities waiting to entertain John Howard and his high society buddies. I run into Bert Newton, who I know well from years of performing on his morning TV show.

'Well, hello, sweetheart,' he pouts, never one to miss an opportunity to camp it up.

We put the final touches to our outfits and soon we're ready to perform. Garry assembles us for a quick chat. He smiles broadly and says, 'I've got something to ask you. The Prime Minister has requested a photo with you all when you've finished your song.'

The group goes quiet. I'm sure there's a bunch of us who'd jump at the opportunity, but I can just *see* the photo. Us, a bunch of 'crazy homosexuals', gathered around a self-consciously grinning PM, 'the people's man', the 'elder statesman', 'friend to all walks of life'. I'm sickened, and I refuse to be a part of that lie.

'No way,' I say. 'I said from the start that I would only do this gig if I didn't have to meet the bastard.'

I look around the group and everyone's gazing at their feet. Dan pipes up.

'Nope. Me neither. I don't wanna do it.'

Garry's smile is wilting. The general consensus is, fittingly, no.

'Okay,' Garry says, the smile returning to his face. 'I'll tell the him you don't want to meet him.' And he spins on a dime and exits. I'm thrilled at the thought that we just snubbed the PM.

We assemble, ready for our entrance. I'm as nervous as hell. This is our debut public performance, our first time in these costumes, and the choreography is at best unfamiliar to me. We look amazing together, and the stragglers from the event who pop out to the toilets stop and remark on how fabulous we are. One impeccably attired woman stops and says condescendingly, 'Oh, look at you. If you're lucky you'll get a photo with the Prime Minister.'

'If we're lucky we won't,' I grumble back.

She physically takes a step backwards, completely stumped. She blinks dumbly for a moment then mutters, 'Well, have a good night then,' and totters back inside, having just met her first Labor voter.

Bert introduces us to the crowd, and the act begins. It passes in a wash of adrenalin, and before we know it we're out the door and back in the dressing room. All the talk on the way up the stairs is about whether we'd seen 'him' and what the expression on his face was like. I realise that I didn't even take a look at him. I'd been so caught up in actually keeping everything together on stage that I'd forgotten he was there.

We're back in at the theatre to start the technical rehearsal after the crew has had the stage for the last forty-eight hours. And that's literally what they've done. They've worked around the clock hanging backdrops, setting lights, timing revolve cues and getting the bus to work. They look like hell, and Garry, who has been here with them, has fallen asleep on the auditorium floor. Simon isn't far off either, but remains in control and cheerful in the face of an increasingly disgruntled crew.

The moment I arrive I'm besieged by wardrobe people, eager to try new shoes and costumes on me. Troy's head is spinning with all the changes, and he can't work out when I wear any of the costumes yet.

We start at the beginning of the show and work through the first act, but soon find there are things that still don't work. They're mostly bus issues. The whole rehearsal grinds to a halt every time the bus has to do anything. The elevators inside the bus are too slow, it seems to stop at will when it's turning, and each time it screws up it takes fifteen to thirty minutes to reset. At times we simply leave an issue unresolved and move on. I feel a pang of panic as I try to second guess when on earth we're actually going to fix these things.

Cam, the head mech, boards the bus during an agonisingly protracted wait and spills what the problem is. It was never designed to work in tandem with the revolve, so the axis of the bus has been shifted to accommodate that. Unfortunately, that means the computer is no longer sure where the bus actually is, so it keeps taking it to the wrong place on stage. The computer guys are trying to reprogram it as we speak, but they can't predict the outcome. This is bad. I hope it's something that is solvable, or we're really screwed. I ask Cam if it can be fixed, and he just shrugs and gives me an exhausted smile.

At this rate, I can't imagine how we'll ever be ready for our first preview in six days.

It's like Groundhog Day. Sunday begins as Saturday ended—we have to wait an hour to start, until the bus is ready to behave herself. What we're waiting for is a cue to get us into the Broken Hill pub scene. The bus rotates as the side closes. We run it a few times, improving the timing each run. What I'm heading for is a quick change into the next scene. It's crucial I time this accurately, but I can't rush it, as the outfit I'm getting into is my thong dress, and the shoes I've been given are literally a foot tall, so there's no way I can run back onto the stage for my entrance. I'll be lucky if I can walk. Troy waits patiently side stage for us to finally get up to where he and another dresser will rip off my previous costume and throw on the next.

Finally, we get there. I leap off the bus and fly through the quick change. I race back to stage as fast as my towering shoes will allow, only to find my entry point blocked by a piece of set that shouldn't be there. My cue to enter comes and goes, and since I'm not on stage everything grinds to a halt.

'I'm here,' I shout feebly. 'I just can't get on stage.' Finally the set flies into the roof and I walk on stage to an ironic round of applause.

'Did you make it?' Simon asks.

'Yep,' I say.

Simon sees the height of my shoes. He's un-amused.

'I want those shoes cut in half', he says. 'He's gonna kill himself in those'.

This is music to my ears.

The day rolls on much the same way, the bus acting up at every opportunity. At one point she runs out of batteries. The crew was up until 4.00 am this morning working her, and the batteries haven't had time to recharge. A giant extension cord is produced from God knows where, and it's slotted into some version of a mains plug. A mechanist is forced to stand on top and guide the power lead around the outside of the bus so it doesn't run over it as it moves. It looks like he's up there driving it himself, like he's got the world's largest remote-control toy.

Patience is at breaking point. Everyone wants to put a bomb under Priscilla-the-bus and blow her into the next musical. The temperature of the chat through the mechanist's headsets is at magma temperature, and several times I see exasperated crew tearing them off, to escape the verbal haranguing. Inside those earpieces, everyone is fighting to be heard as they attempt to fix the myriad of problems that bombard them.

It's not just the bus, it's the timing of flys, the timing of the revolve, the constant absence of pieces of set or costume. Lighting hasn't had time to focus lights, so action is in darkness, and we have to stop until lighting has caught up. It's a world of hurt, and the weekend can't come fast enough for everyone.

As actors, we have to stand around and wait until each problem is sorted out. My overwhelming preference is to be on this side of the headsets, and I retreat into a Zen-like State, making a concerted effort to project patience and goodwill. The last thing anyone needs is a testy actor huffing at how fucked up everything is. But utter confusion reigns. No one can answer the simplest of questions, because no one can second-guess how long any single problem will take to be solved.

By the end of the day we seem to be approaching the end of act one. We hit the dialogue scene before the closing number of the act, and just as my belief surges that we'll really, truly make it, Kath steps on stage and calls, 'Time.'

Simon crumples. We all crumple. Couldn't we just stay and finish? This is impossible, because we all know it's highly likely that we'd still be here at 5.00 am. Aside from that, the crew are already heading off to get extremely drunk.

My day off seems to fly by. The kids want to know where the hell I've been all this time. How do you explain to a couple of kids who are used to their dad being constantly at hand that he's been at *WORK?* A strange and unfamiliar concept.

I sleep like the dead, and soon find myself back at the theatre for more of the same. Simon has the day in Melbourne for MTC business today, so I spend the morning rehearsing quick changes with Troy. Nearly all of my many costumes have to be changed at light speed. To be sure I'm back on time they need to be rehearsed like a dance number. First we lay out what I have to get into, and then we prepare what I'll be coming out of. We step through it slowly, making sure we have the procedure correct. Then we go through it at speed. We click a stopwatch and go for it. I race in from stage and throw off my gear. Troy holds out pieces of costumes for me, and I get into them. The shirts have been dressed with Velcro, so there are no buttons to negotiate. The shoes have elastic laces, so I just pull them on. Once I've finished I race back to the stage.

'Twenty seconds,' Troy says victoriously. We've done it. This change will work. We go through all the fast changes this way, sorting whether we need extra help. The Gumby change will require three dressers, all going like the clappers. I strip and Troy puts on my pants and shoes as another puts on my make-up mask and enormous headpiece, as another applies lipstick. As we bash through it I feel like the latest model Commodore as it travels along the production line. Panels on, windscreen fitted, roof lowered, and I'm away. Troy looks at the stopwatch. We made it.

Today we're supposed to shoot the TV ad and have the program shots taken, but again the stage has been given over to the long suffering crew, so that they can keep attending to problems and catching up with their enormous workload.

They only have until the evening, at which time we'll continue the tech run. We finally make it through to the end of the act. It feels like an amazing victory. It has taken seven days. Now we have three days to finish the second act before our first preview on Friday night. I already know this is completely impossible.

It's Wednesday morning, and I'm in early for a publicity call. Strangely, getting into drag make-up is beginning to feel run of the mill. I no longer find the need to grab a camera and snap the strange creature in the mirror. We head to the stage, and the reaction of the photographer to our 'get-up' reminds me of how awesome this show must look when you're not in here, day in, day out. I make a mental note to keep it fresh and not tire of what is so impressive about this show.

After lunch we pick up the tech rehearsal again at the top of act two. This scene runs into the Les Girls number. It requires a quick change for the male ensemble to get into their extraordinary costumes and headpieces, as well as a huge set change where an enormous staircase appears out of nowhere. We try it once, and of course no one makes it. It's a disaster. The cast are gobsmacked at how heavy the headpieces are and how dangerous the walk down the staircase is.

We have to go again, but it all takes time to reset— about an hour. The second time it almost works, and that's enough for Simon. We push on into 'Shake Your Groove Thing', finding we have no costumes or shoes for the number, only incredibly heavy headpieces. It beggars belief that if the wardrobe department knew we had to wear these things on our heads *and* dance in them, why they'd make them so heavy. We suck it up and continue with the number, but I see Dan boiling beneath the surface. We've only got two days until preview. Will we even have our costumes by then?

Tony has fared the worst. He has almost no costumes. Most have been thrown out or modified, and the wardrobe department has been working furiously to try and get their replacements ready. Subsequently, Tony and his dresser are at a loss over which costumes he should be wearing when, and they still haven't rehearsed any quick changes. In one scene he misses his entry altogether, and Dan and I wait for him to appear on stage so we can begin the scene. When he finally makes it, he limps onto stage a defeated man, his dresser nursing a bruised eye where Tony has unwittingly kneed him during the panic of the quick change.

We move on again, but things are still not completely

teched in the scene. It's a terrible worry, as I can't imagine when we're actually going to get time to smooth all this stuff out.

The lighting is magnificent though. Not since Alice Cooper, Festival Hall, 1977, have I seen so many lights hung in one place.

When the lights are about to change colour, the coloured gels must roll into their new position first. Because there's so many of them rolling at once, they sound like a huge flock of birds simultaneously breaking into flight. These are the kind of things one contemplates as one waits hour after hour for something to happen.

As the day approaches its end, and I'm feeling like we're getting through a lot of stuff, Cam approaches clutching his tech sheets.

'Know how many pages are on my tech sheet?' he asks. 'Ten for the entire show. Know how many we've done?'

I dread the answer.

'Six,' he says. 'That means there's four to go, and two days to do it.'

He saunters off shaking his head to the heavens and smiling a mad, defeated smile.

We continue to work those four pages on Thursday. We all know the drill very well by now. Everything is such a mess that it's pointless getting upset. Everyone is stretched. Everyone is exhausted. Everyone is working their guts out. I feel like Kurtz at the end of the river in *Heart of Darkness*. I now accept that our first preview will be a terrible disaster, and I'm preparing myself for that. That things are going to go wrong is a given. The horror, the horror.

All I can do now is put my twenty-five years of experience in the theatre to work and come up with something on Friday night that vaguely resembles a performance. There have been worse dilemmas in the trenches, for God's sake. We're only going on stage.

By the end of the day we've only made it to the

performance at the Alice Springs casino, about three quarters of the way through the show. None of the smoothing out that needed to be done has been done, and the memory of act one is nothing but a distant glimmer on the horizon. We only have tomorrow to finish teching the show before the preview that night.

When we finish the day, an exhausted Simon gathers us and tells us he's a deer in the headlights. He's run out of options and must send us on stage tomorrow night whether he likes it or not, even though the show is not yet ready. He says tomorrow is a must do commitment. We'll be honest with the house and say we're not ready. We'll implore them to bear with us.

Garry joins him and tells us we're cancelling the Sunday and Wednesday matinee shows so we can continue getting the show right. All these cancellations means they're taking an enormous financial hit, as well as the potential fall out in the media that *Priscilla, Queen of the Desert, The Musical* is going straight to hell. Talk has already started. He implores us to keep a lid on what we say 'out there' about what's happening.

'It's crucial that we don't look like we're panicking,' he says. 'The media will pounce on us like a pack of dogs and kill us. Just say our tech rehearsals are taking longer than we anticipated, which is kinda the truth.' He smiles an exhausted but cheeky smile. Somehow, these two have managed to keep their sense of humour through everything.

We break for the night knowing that the weekend will now entail three shows and more teching on Sunday.

Friday arrives. A focus comes over us all, which has previously escaped us. We know each time we move on with the tech that it gets us closer to the end and gives us a little more that we can show to the audience. We get to a stage in the show where we no longer need the bus, and everyone breathes a sigh of relief about that, but we don't actually get to the end.

This is bad, as the end of the show involves sending Tony, Dan, and me up on a scissor lift to stand on top of the bus to sing 'We Belong'. We'll just have to wing this tonight under work lights. Being afraid of heights, I'm not relishing this at all.

We go to the meal break with our heads swimming with thousands of tiny pieces of information which, grouped together, will become *Priscilla, Queen of the Desert, the Musical*. I'm sure there are hundreds of things I've forgotten, and I know beyond anything that tonight I'm going to need to be sharp as a tack.

Chapter 16
First Preview

Picture one of those dreams where you're about to go on stage to sing with The Rolling Stones, but you can't remember any of the lyrics, and you don't have any pants on. After a lifetime of having such dreams, one is actually occurring. Surprisingly, I'm not that nervous. I'm so convinced that the performance we're about to give will be an unmitigated disaster that I've given myself over to the experience before it's even happened. I will forge a path of good humour through the constant stream of adversity and through all the madness. I have reorganised my brain into damage control mode. At the five-minute-call I tap at Tony's dressing room door and quietly ask how he feels about riffing with the audience if things go wrong.

'Oh, no,' he shoots back. 'No, that's not what I do. I'm not comfortable with that at all.'

'Okay,' I say. 'Then I won't pull you into it unless you want to join in, but if things fall apart I'm going to reach out to them.'

We embrace each other as if we're about to go into battle, which in this case is not such an extreme analogy. I tap at Dan's door. He looks up at me and gives me an anxious giggle, like he's just set eyes on the decrepit rope bridge over which he's been commanded to cross at gunpoint. We hug. There's little to say. Through the Tannoy we can hear the audience filling the auditorium. It's a sold out performance, almost two thousand expectant punters, most of them gay, eagerly anticipating the first ever performance of this show.

'Act one beginners,' is called, and I take a deep breath and head to side stage. 'Chookas,' I call to anyone I pass on the way, but my concentration is not on individuals now, more important is the mass of lines, songs, blocking, quick changes, dance routines, and potential failures ahead of me over the next three hours. I stand side stage and think through my path for the first ten minutes of the show. I try to breathe in the feeling of being Tick.

Simon is side stage, more nervous than me. We catch each other's eye, and he gives me one of his boyish grins. His smile carries more than its fair share of apprehension. Kath gives him a nod, and Simon steps on stage.

The murmur of the huge crowd instantly turns to applause. We gather around the stage management monitor to watch, our hearts in our mouths at what he's about to say. He gestures for them to hush and let him speak.

'Good evening,' he begins. 'I'm Simon Phillips, the director of what you are about to see.' The crowd erupts into applause again. 'Thanks for that, but you mightn't want to applaud me after what I'm about to tell you. As you're all aware this is a brand new show. And with that comes certain challenges. We're not entirely finished rehearsing it, but rather than cancelling the show, what you are about to see tonight is a rare glimpse into the making of a theatrical production.' The crowd cheer again.

166

'Aren't you lucky?' They all laugh. 'So it's not a matter of *if* the show grinds to a halt, it's a matter of *when*, how many times and *how long* it will grind to a halt for.'

He begs them to bear with us and to be as encouraging as possible to the poor actors, whose miserable job it is to muck through what is bound to be a difficult night.

With that said the band strikes up the overture. I get a stab of nerves, which I try to swipe away.

The curtain goes up, and the show begins. The Divas fly in from the roof, and the crowd hoots. 'Downtown' begins, and the ensemble throws themselves into it. I jog up and down on the spot behind the flitter curtain, waiting for my cue. One moment at a time, I tell myself. It's a game of tennis. Play each point as it comes.

Filled with adrenalin, I make my first entry, and I get my first glimpse of the auditorium filled with people. It's an impressive sight. I try to put it out of my mind and focus on what I'm doing. So far so good. Nothing has gone wrong. We're thirty seconds into the show. Before I know it the song is finished, and I'm backstage doing my quick change into my 'Never Been To Me' costume. I can't believe we haven't stopped yet. I race to get to my entrance, and I make it. I stand atop a platform adorned with footlights, and I'm rolled manually onto the stage for my entrance. The crowd gasp at the final picture of Tick in drag as I push through the flitter curtain. I'm tottery in my stiletto heels under my emerald dress, and when the mechanists pushing reach the end point of the platform's track (which is beyond the end of the stage and over the orchestra pit), they stop all too abruptly. I overbalance and almost fall straight into the pit. Being afraid of heights I totally shit myself, and my legs begin to shake uncontrollably. I can barely stand. I breathe through the panic and try to focus on miming the song, wondering if the audience can sense my terror. The end of the routine can't come quickly enough, and I race backstage for my next change, cursing and breathing deep calming breaths as I go.

Miraculously, the show continues uninterrupted for about forty minutes. There is, of course, the odd clunky moment, which we professionally ignore, but there hasn't been a terrible car accident yet.

Then it happens.

The bus stops for some reason, and the three queens are marooned on stage with nothing to do but grin sheepishly. Simon's voice booms over the sound system. 'Sorry, folks, we have a problem.'

Dan retreats to the bus and Tony hovers. I walk to the edge of the stage and begin a sing-a-long of 'Kumbaya My Lord'. Audiences love it when things go wrong, and this is no exception. They've been waiting all night for this to happen, and finally they're getting a taste of the chaos Simon had promised. I have no intention of letting them down.

'Hello, up there,' I say waving at those in 'the gods'. 'Who do we have up there? All the drag queens and the lesbians. Hello, guys.' They laugh and wave back. 'And what about down the front here in the stalls? We've got all the John Howard supporters.' There's a big laugh, followed by a nasty hiss. 'Oh, dear! Never do political jokes, huh?'

The bus is soon fixed and we travel on. Amazingly, we make it to the end of act one with few problems. I retreat to my dressing room to regroup. Across the hall, Tony is madly fixing make-up and getting into his second act costume. I sit for a moment and try to calm myself.

The second act is diabolical. There are constant stoppages, and props appear at bizarre times and in bizarre places. Tony and I find ourselves once again marooned onstage during a stoppage. By this time, Tony has joined in the riffing, and our chatting to the audience has become a given, which they eagerly look forward to. Simon makes another announcement about a stoppage and speculates whether Tony and I have run out of stand up material yet.

'Simon's terrified I'll make another John Howard joke,' I say. 'Oh, by the way, did you hear we did a publicity gig in front of our Prime Minister?'

'He wanted a photo with us,' Tony says.

'We said no,' I boast bitchily.

The crowd laughs and applauds. When they fall silent again, Tony quips casually, 'When *he* does something for us, *we'll* do something for *him*.'

This brings the roof down. The audience howls with laughter. I think back to what he said in the dressing room before the show. 'It's not what I do.' *Indeed!*

When we finally limp to the end of the show, we find it has taken us over four hours to get through, and the audience has supported us generously the entire way. We're now totally exhausted, and so are they. As I'm taking off my make-up, Sandra appears and reminds me that there's a party in the show room for the audience, which I'm invited to. 'Of course I know you'll want to go home, but I just thought I'd let you know,' she says.

As much as I desperately want to go home, I feel beholden to this fabulous crowd who have been so generous to us tonight. I need to go to the party and thank them.

I enter the show room to find a party in full swing. As I push towards the stage, everyone I pass thanks me for the show and tells me how fabulous it was. I can't believe it. It felt completely chaotic.

Mitzi Macintosh hits the stage and introduces the few members of the cast who have shown up. We assemble on stage. I snatch the mic from her and thank the audience for their generosity.

'There's no way we could have got through the show tonight without your beautiful support. Thank you.'

Again they cheer generously. There is a genuine sense of excitement amongst them that they were a part of something tonight—that they witnessed some kind of history in the making, and I guess they did. Messy, fucked up, tentative, but performed with gusto and heart. The show is finally on the stage.

Chapter 17
Second and Third Previews

As I arrive at the theatre for the second preview, I reassure myself that if you've base jumped once it can't possibly be as bad the second time. Wrong. The temperature on stage as I pass heading to my dressing room is hot. The dance of the vandalised ants nest has returned. Something bad has happened. My heart sinks.

I scan the chaos for an authoritative face and find Kath. She gives me a sympathetic smile and tells me the bus has broken down. Whatever a current converter is, it's failed and the bus won't work. I wait for the four beautiful words, 'You can go home,' but they don't come. In their place I hear, but don't quite believe, 'We're doing the show without it.' Did *The Phantom of the Opera* go on without the chandelier? Did *Miss Saigon* go on without the helicopter? Did *Hair* go on without clothes? The answer to all these question is probably yes, so in our second public outing we'll go on without Priscilla. We'll be base jumping without the parachute today.

I tap on Tony's door, and he looks up at me from his make-up mirror in mock horror. We can do little but chuckle. Dan appears, and we have a quick discussion about how to mime a bus. Quick changes have been set in the bus too. We have to reassign where we'll be doing them. Characters appear through the roof of the bus via the elevators inside. How will we do that? The truth is there are so many points at which the bus is crucial that the only practical way to do this show is to make it up as we go along.

Garry and Simon arrive. When things go badly, Garry's smile tends to widen, although his eyes don't necessarily smile with them. Simon giggles nervously alongside him. They try to reassure us that everything will be all right, but they're both so tired that nothing comprehensible spills out. The measure of this disaster can be nothing but an enormous joke. It's almost like it's not happening.

As dressers scramble around us trying to replot their change points, and stage management and props people scan the show for places where the whole thing could come unstuck, we three queens know that the success or failure of this adventure is again resting squarely on our shoulders.

I retreat to my dressing room to once again gather myself for the coming onslaught. I begin the process of re-programming my brain to cheerfully take whatever happens today on the chin and try to enjoy it. This is a story for the grandkids. I get made up and put on my first costume.

At beginners, Simon is again standing nervously side stage. Garry has decided to give the whole audience free tickets to another show as a sweetener. This will cost him a fortune, as it's another full house. Simon hits the stage and tells the audience the bad news.

'Never in my life have I worked with such a prima donna,' he says about the bus. 'She's gone into her dressing room, and she won't come out.' He butters the audience up beautifully, and by the time the overture begins they are one hundred percent with us.

All goes reasonably smoothly up until the point in 'Go West' where Felicia gestures to the flitter curtain, which then rises to reveal the bus. Tick and Bernadette reel in shock that he's bought a bus, and the three queens circle it in awe. Of course today there's nothing there. We pretend the bus has appeared and do our choreography as writ. When we arrive back to the front of the stage Felicia says, 'What do you think?' I turn my next line to our advantage and say, 'When do we have to get this *imaginary bus* back to the school?' The audience crack up laughing, and from then on entirely go with the notion that for the rest of the afternoon they'll be imagining the bus with us.

We muck through absolutely everything. If the bus has to turn, we turn. If it rotates, we rotate. One of us mocks holding an imaginary steering wheel, while the others do the scene on the bare stage pretending we're sitting in our life-sized bus. It's shambolic, but again the audience is tolerant and supportive and at the end of the show gives us a standing ovation for our troubles.

Bathed in sweat, we finish the show and bolt for the sanctuary of our dressing rooms. We have to repeat this marathon tonight, so in the meantime I intend to eat and sleep and avoid any kind of communication with other human beings.

The night show runs the same way as the afternoon show, but with a larger and rowdier crowd. We're slightly more adept at knowing what to do in the absence of a bus, and technical hitches, which were slowing the show down in all of the previous previews, are getting ironed out. Effectively we're tech running the show in front of our audiences. This is great for the crew, but a huge worry for the actors. I'm becoming aware that I'm still not focusing on improving my own performance, because my mind has to be so aware of the constant stream of technical issues. Previews are traditionally shows to test how the audience is responding to jokes and scenes, and to hone your performance. This is not happening at all for me, and I long for everything to be set so I can begin this process.

Sunday's matinee has been cancelled, so we can continue teching the show. We drag ourselves back into the theatre at eleven. I arrive to find that the wrong current converter was sent from Adelaide, so the bus is *still* not working. This means that we can't tech anything involved with the bus. There's so much stuff to do that no one seems to know where to start. A strange listlessness pervades the entire work force, including the usually resilient Simon. I find myself doing a lot of standing around, while others drag themselves reluctantly through cues they would rather not be bothered with. Everyone wants the show to be fixed, but we're all too exhausted and have lost the will to fix it.

At the end of the day the cast, at least, head home for a day off. I guess that the crew will have another long day in here tomorrow, and will have to work through their weekend, poor sods. At least they don't have to put a public face on the world of chaos that's spinning out of control backstage. The kind of white lie we've been selling our audiences for the last three shows takes an enormous toll, and I head home completely shattered. I want to sleep for a year.

Chapter 18
Hell
Final Week

It's about 4.00 am on Tuesday morning. The fog of a slightly putrid dream begins to curl into my now increasingly restless sleep. In this dream, someone is taking to the inside of my throat with a knife. I fight them off, but I'm weak in my bed, and my assailant is cunning. I thrash around until I'm disconnected from my sleep enough to stir, and then wake.

When I finally hit consciousness, I sit bolt upright in bed and clutch at my throat. It stings. The Perp' has flown the apartment, but he's left behind his nasty infliction. I swallow hard against the pain, thinking it may ease it, but the sharp sting only serves to rouse me further.

I squint through the gathering dawn light to the clock. My guts turn slightly as I see I've only got a few hours before I have to be back at the theatre. I know only too well what a sore throat means at this stage of the game. This is day one of the final week leading up to opening night. Ground zero is upon us. The final stages of technical rehearsals, and the last few previews, are now the only things standing between us and the curtain going up for the world premiere on Saturday night.

In my mind's eye I can picture the moment: me, standing side stage amongst the flap of nervous performers, nervous myself, feeling the cling of fishnets and the crush of the corset beneath my overcoat, ready for my first entrance. The rippling murmur from the audience as it flows through the curtain from the auditorium. Then an excited crescendo as the house lights die and the orchestra stabs at the first few bars of the overture.

It's a scene that bristles with excitement and fear and adrenalin. It's akin to giving birth in the sense that after gestating this thing in rehearsals, suffering the misgivings and uncertainties of putting your heart and soul into a performance, then finally the agony of the overwhelming nerves, we deliver the show to the world, wide-eyed and innocent for all to scrutinise and critique.

Every piece of publicity insists on billing it as 'the world premiere' of *Priscilla, Queen of the Desert, The Musical*, as if calling it opening night isn't enough to make you fill your brown corduroys. But now this niggling sore throat that I've been keeping at bay for two weeks has decided to sink its teeth in at the worst possible time. I need all my health and all my strength because the week ahead is going to be big.

Once daylight comes, I fly down to the doctor's and demand antibiotics. As I wait for my prescription to be filled, I trot down the aisles in the chemists, filling my basket with vitamins as though I'm on an Easter egg hunt. I open a prodigious account of pills, potions and remedies.

I return home and report to Annie. She's been holding the fort for the last two weeks with our little terrors, both of whom seem to be coming down with what I've got. As I'm trying to elicit as much sympathy as possible, the phone rings, and Sandra stuns me with the news that Judith Johnson, our extraordinary publicist, has died. This is the kind of enormous news that puts everything else into perspective, and I go easy on the self-pity. Although her death was unforeseeable and unrelated to the show, it's hard not to feel like *Priscilla* has claimed her first scalp.

I head into work. In a terrible twist of irony, today we're scheduled to shoot the TV ad. This has been organised by Judith, and in her absence her grieving assistant must suck it up and hold the fort. Aside from all the technical difficulties backstage, there is now a sizable group of people in serious mourning for Judith. She's been a theatre stalwart for years, and a lot of people around me were very close to her, so the atmosphere is fractious. Aside from this, we're rudderless. Simon is in Melbourne presiding over the launch of the next MTC season, so we have no real leader.

We assemble to start work on the ad, but it seems utterly insane to be shooting it in favour of actually getting the show up and running. We keep looking to each other askance that this folly is continuing. Surely we should stop right now and finish teching the bloody show.

The list of the routines we'll be shooting are pinned up on the noticeboard, and we make our way through each as the day progresses. Impressive camera equipment is set up in the auditorium, and we run each number a couple of times for the benefit of the camera.

Gradually we get behind time, and the last few numbers begin to become rushed. Tempers fray, and the workload expected finally defeats us. We cut several scheduled scenes, and the ad director is forced to make do with what he's got.

After a quick meal break, we get ready for another preview. Ten minutes before the curtain goes up we're assembled on stage and informed that the bus has broken down again. Once more we'll have to perform without it. I look around and see the cast's patience and sense of humour has almost run out. My throat is deteriorating, and I ache to be home in bed. We muck through the show as best as we can, but my anxiety about actually being ready for opening night is soaring.

Wednesday, and when I arrive at the theatre today I find my dressing room packed with suit bags. Last week I tracked down Fernando (can you hear the drums?) and asked him to dress me for the opening night party. Aside from an aversion to shopping, I also knew I wouldn't have a second to actually find anything to wear. With all the hype, and the thousands of press there, I didn't want to turn up looking like a hobo.

For a fee, Fernando would do all the shopping for me. I could simply choose the outfit I wanted, send back what I didn't need, and keep the rest. I just didn't count on an avalanche of clothing coming into my already clogged dressing room. I now have more suits and shirts than actual costumes.

The brief I gave him was masculine. If I'm going to be dressed like a girl on stage all night, I want to go to the party dressed like a man. Perhaps the message didn't get through, because as I flick through the outfits I see a hell of a lot of floral. Troy, who also happens to be a NIDA trained designer, helps me chose which suits me best. It's not hard. One outfit is perfect, and we settle on that pretty quickly.

Today is another exhausting day of technical rehearsals, breathing acrid smoke machine fumes, and is capped off with a preview. As the day wears on I can feel my voice getting weaker and more compromised. The infection is moving to my chest, and it's now become painful to cough. My sense of humour has run out.

The show is still chaotic. Although the bus is working again, for the last three shows we've been doing quick changes in the wings or in bizarre alternative places, so to readjust to using the bus will be a major shift. Of course the bus is still not teched properly, so her moves around the stage are clunky, and we still have to do a lot of filling in. I'm deeply tired and getting very sick of keeping everything together. It's also still unpredictable where and when props will turn up, if they turn up at all.

In the dressing room scene in Woop Woop, I spend the entire scene getting dressed on stage ready for the song that follows. I slip on boots, put on lipstick and glitter, a skirt and then my headpiece. All of this is timed to fit into the dialogue. Every single night we've performed the scene, the props and costume have been set in different places, so not only have I had to play the scene, I've had to assess where everything actually is and then work out how to get into it, all in the time appointed before the song starts. Tonight when I pick up my headpiece to put it on, the make shift costume rack that the props department have made for it overbalances and crashes to the stage. It's the last fucking straw. The audience laugh at how clumsy it looks, but I've had a gut full. Normally I'd use it and make a wise crack to the audience, but feeling so sick and so exhausted I'm in no mood for any more stuff ups. I stare down at the mess on the stage in front of me and wrestle with the overwhelming desire to scream and stomp off stage. I decide to simply ignore it and let it be someone else's problem. For all I care, whoever is responsible for leaving me on stage with such a crappy set up can come on and sort it out. I can't be bothered anymore. But this is still the real world. On stage, actors rule and any mess must be cleaned up by them. Backstage crew have the luxury of peeking anonymously through the wings at their mistakes.

I turn my back on the toppled costume rack and continue dressing and playing the scene as if nothing has happened. Dan quickly makes light of it and rushes to clean it up, and the audience cackles. I'm grateful, but in my fury I dearly wish he hadn't. For once I ached for a red-faced crew member to be forced on stage, just to see how it feels.

Desperate for rest, I bolt home straight after the show for a decent night's sleep, and I'm out as soon as I hit the pillow. After about thirty minutes though, it's as if some mad scientist has pulled down a giant electrical conducting lever as my heart suddenly bursts into life and begins to pound heavily in my chest. My eyes pop open, and I sit bolt upright. In my slumber I've had a horrifying realisation. I'm going to lose my voice for opening night! I'm awash with panic, and I can't calm down. Scenarios of failure whirl through my mind.

For hours I sweat and spin circles in bed. Finally my restlessness stirs Annie and she mutters, 'What's wrong?'

I'm forced to confess that I'm having a panic attack and so can't sleep. She takes me in her arms and strokes my head. I immediately feel a million times better, until at around 4.00 am when the kids wake up crying. Their temperatures have soared, and their throats are killing them too. Now everyone's awake.

I sit on the side of the bed with my head in my hands as the kids scream, groaning with despair at the disaster that is about to confront me.

It's Thursday. I stagger in to work knowing I have to admit to the company that I'm in trouble. So much shit is going down backstage that I'm afraid that I'll just present as a nuisance. I summon Simon to my dressing room and unburden myself about what's happening. I tell him I haven't slept, that I'm feeling crook as a dog, and that I'm in a state of panic about not making it to opening night. Tears tumble out as I speak. Simon is shouldering the excruciating burden of ironing out all the disasters of the show, and the pressure is showing. The last thing he needs is to know that one of his leads is crumbling. As I speak, I see all the possible scenarios tumbling around in his mind. He keeps a kind face, but there's clearly minimal bandwidth left in his busy head to deal with this. He assures me he'll go easy on me today, and he exits, telling me to get some rest. I lie on the couch in my dressing room and try to sleep.

Soon, Sandra barrels into my room with a headful of steam. Word has passed around, and she's swung into action. A hotel room has been booked for tonight so I can get some sleep away from the sick kids. Garry arrives with a handful of sleeping pills—lovely, light blue and terribly tempting—to make sure nothing can go wrong for a good night of reviving sleep. I want to gobble the lot and sleep for a week. I can't wait.

Today we have a giant press call before we begin tech rehearsals. Terence Stamp has arrived from London and will perform a 'handing over of the stiletto' ceremony for the cameras.

We get into costume and make-up and assemble side stage waiting to perform a number for the waiting media. The auditorium is filled with TV crews, radio crews, newspaper photographers and journalists. Garry takes to the stage and addresses them, introducing the number we'll do, and promising them we'll do it twice so the cameras can get a different angle. He'll then throw the cast open for them to talk to.

We hit the stage and perform the song. Cameras flash and TV cameras roll. We get to the end of the number, and there's polite applause. We reset and repeat the number. This time the cameras are closer, running up to the stage, trying for a better angle. At the end of the number, our new publicist, Peter, grabs various cast members for interviews. I'm hustled off for an ABC radio interview. We sit in the auditorium and share an impressive looking microphone as we chat cheerfully about why the show is going to be such a hit.

Then it's Terence Stamp's turn. It's amazing what a difference an international star makes to the care factor of the media. What was a polite, run-of-the-mill press call suddenly becomes a frenzy. The press flood to the front of the auditorium, jockeying for a good position, as Terence appears, looking almost self-consciously casual, wearing a faded Hawaiian shirt and a pair of shorts, like he's some old bloke from Maroubra. He's clearly used to the fuss that's made of him, and he gracefully takes it in his stride. He waits backstage with Tony and Dan and me, making polite chit-chat about the show and telling funny anecdotes about the film.

He walks on stage to thunderous applause, carrying with him the stiletto that he will pass to Tony. Tony enters, beaming, and the cameras flash.

'I hereby pass this stiletto on to the new Bernadette,' Terence says, handing the shoe to Tony and giving him a kiss on the cheek. The kiss lingers so the cameras can get their shot.

After a few more interviews, the place empties, and we get back to teching the show. It's still miles off being ready. There are only two previews to go, and we haven't yet done a show without stopping. Costumes and sets are still missing, and we haven't done a dress rehearsal. Every time I think of presenting what we've got on opening night, a shiver of dread grips me.

After rehearsals and a short meal break, I struggle through the show and then slink away into the night, retreating to the Medina Grand in the centre of Sydney. I present at reception in the middle of the night like some kind of eccentric recluse. No luggage, no overnight bags, just a plastic supermarket bag filled with pill bottles, which rattle and clink as I walk.

I make my way to the lift and my new sanctuary on the eighteenth floor. Once the lift doors close behind me I test out how my voice feels after the show, making strange "Scooby Doo" doggie noises across the highs and lows of my vocal range. So absorbed am I with this analysis that I don't notice the lift stop at level three and let in a young, happy newlywed couple. I look up to find them staring bug eyed at me as I make my insane guttural noises. I cease immediately, but it's too late. They've heard me. It's now become a very slow ride to the eighteenth floor as the bride and groom sincerely worry they may not see out their honeymoon before they're filleted by the crazy guy in the lift.

Once ensconced in my refuge, I pop a sleeping pill, tuck myself under the crispy clean sheets and wait for the magic sleep to roll in. It finally comes, but my temperature is up, and I keep waking in sweat-drenched sheets.

At about 4.00 am I wake and I can't get back to sleep. This time I can tell there's no use trying. I get up and pace the hotel room butt naked, trying to shake off my excruciating, irrational fear. I open the curtains and stare into the peaceful darkness, cursing the internal chaos that assaults me. Is this how it will be on opening night—staring out through the curtain to the still, watchful crowd as I wrestle on stage with this turmoil?

A thought hits me. I'm making myself sicker by worrying about being sick. In my feverish, sleep-deprived panic, I realise that what I need to do is to have someone magically remove this evil barrier to my recovery. In a flash of inspiration, I pounce on the Yellow Pages and look up hypnotists. This is brilliant! A hypnotist will hypnotise the sickness away and stop the panic. I find a hypnotist with the closest city address and tear the page from the phone book, safe in the assumption that any future guests are highly unlikely to want a quick visit to the hypnotist whilst on their stay in Sydney. It's four thirty, and I resolve to call the hypnotist as soon as the clock hits eight. Knowing I'm now saved, I go back to bed.

Dead on 8.00 am I dial the number from the Yellow Pages. In one of the more unforgettable phone calls of my life, I explain my unusual story and plead with the hypnotist to see me at short notice. For a moment I think she's going to have me committed, or simply hang up, but something about the desperation in my voice catches in her distant, medical-student drive to help the sick and despairing, and she agrees to see me at eleven thirty, emphasising strongly that this is her day off. Convinced I'm saved I go back to bed.

When I wake again I feel even sicker. I'm due at the theatre at 10.00 am for interviews, followed by more technical rehearsals, followed by a preview. There's no way I'll get through today, so I text Sandra to say I won't be coming in for the press call, and then I turn off my phone.

I buy flowers to take as a peace offering for destroying my shrink's day off, and jump into a cab for my appointment. Of all the taxis in Sydney, I choose the chirp-a-chirp-a-cheep-cheep cab. The driver is so overwhelmed with the desire to spread his chit-chatty good cheer to the world that he doesn't notice the seething, cross-armed lump of misery in the back seat. I find myself willing my sickness to somehow download itself from me and attach itself to him, just so he'll shut-the-fuck-up. Because it's my shrink's day off, I'm forced to endure him for a good forty minutes while we travel over hill and dale to her home, out in some far-reaching suburb with a name that sounds like a reality TV show.

He finally drops me at a newly carved crescent, which, unlike my life at present, is perfectly ordered and boasts not a shrub, lamp pole or fence post out of place. I check the address and buzz for my shrink. She emerges from her condo, obviously wary, and takes me in. I give her the flowers and she does her professional best not to blush.

Cheerfully making chit-chat, she leads me through her immaculately tidy sand-washed apartment to her home consulting room. I sit on luxurious cushions, trying not to betray the depths of my embarrassment about the tale I'm about to unfold. She looks at me with plastered encouragement, like I truly am a maniac and things can only go up hill from here. Thankfully, she has no idea about the theatre, what the show is, or who I am. Either this or she's doing a fabulous snow job.

I unpack my misery before her, and she listens intently, her eyes never leaving mine until I've run out of neuroses to offer her. She warns me not to expect miracles, that I'll probably feel like we're just talking while I'm under.

She counts down from ten to one, instructing me to relax. She taps my forehead and speaks in gentle tones. When I'm finally supposed to be under I still feel just like me, plopped on a comfy couch answering questions. I do indeed feel like we're just talking. I'm certain it hasn't worked or I've somehow screwed up, but as the session progresses and we begin to cover some important ground, I put my doubts aside and co-operate. We spend nearly two hours together as she takes me to unexpected places, away from what I imagined was really going on.

When the session finishes, I truly feel like things have changed somehow. I head for the door, thanking her profusely. She leaves me to wait for a cab back to the hotel. On the way, I stop at a chemist and buy a product that promises to break up the mucus on my chest. I slurp the stuff before reading the caution on the label that warns it may cause diarrhoea. This is, of course, what immediately happens.

It's now late Friday afternoon. Opening night is one sleep away. World War III would have to break out for it not to happen, but as I lie here, prostrate across the sofa, I don't know how I'm going to even make it on stage tonight. Sooner or later I have to resurface and make the decision of whether I can physically get through the show.

That's when I turn on my phone and seconds later it rings.

'Jeremy?' Sandra says breathlessly. 'I think I've got something here that could help you. We have a nurse in at the theatre giving out Vitamin B injections. Would you like one?'

My plea is answered. I've had a Vitamin B shot before,

and they're miracle workers. Kids, don't mess with drugs, just go straight for the Vitamin B shot. I drag myself off the couch and head into the theatre with the promise of getting my hit.

I stumble into the nurse's room just as she's packing up.

'One more,' I blurt as I barrel past her and present my arm like an eager junkie.

'Other end,' she quips, and I lower my jeans. To take my mind off the jab I scan the room for things to distract me and notice the empty syringe receptacle brimming with needles. Clearly, I'm not the only member of the cast or crew seeking salvation.

Afterwards, I head upstairs, and by the time I reach my dressing room, whether it's a placebo or not, I'm already feeling the effects of the shot. Energy begins to return to my depleted soul. I do my best to keep a low profile, choosing to greet Tony and Dan only. I shut my dressing room door against the buzz of what will be the final preview before opening night tomorrow.

Kath knocks gently at my door and asks how I'm feeling. I tell her I'm not great, but I don't go into any detail. She fills me in on what they did in the tech today, most of it being tidying up work, which won't affect me directly. I'm so pleased I didn't come in.

I make-up and enter a routine of gargling and pill popping. I warm my voice and body up and mentally prepare. By the time the curtain rises, I've somehow managed to gather enough will and energy to feel like going on stage.

'Downtown' begins, and I launch myself into the show, determined not to stop until it finishes. Parts of it are still clunky and uncertain, but the audience reaction is unequivocal. They roar their approval at the bows, and give us a heartfelt standing ovation. It encourages me that perhaps we will get across the line tomorrow night. After all the toil and the anguish, we bloody well deserve to.

I race to my dressing room and get changed at lightning speed. I've kept the hotel room on in case I still feel like crashing there tonight. Annie has given her blessing that I should, so I hunt down a cab and arrive back to sanctuary for my last chance to sleep off this bitch of a flu before we open tomorrow night.

Chapter 19

Opening Night

October 7th, 2006

My eyes pop open at 8.00 am. As I reorient myself, I realise I've slept the entire night. No waking in pools of sweat, no panic attacks. Maybe my shrink has pulled it off. I gingerly slip out of bed and test how I feel. The bad news is that I still feel crook, but the good news is that I've had some sleep.

Today is a legitimate day off. The cast hasn't been called in to the theatre until the hour call, the first time in two weeks they haven't worked us day and night. I'm determined to get back to Coogee and see the family. I call Annie and let her know I'm on my way.

'Are you sure?' she says tenderly. 'Stay there and rest if you need to.' I tell her I need to be with them today.

I hit the glare of a brilliant Sydney morning. People are beginning to bustle around the narrow streets. I ache to be one of them, just an anonymous person racing to get their shopping in for the week, not a quivering, self-indulgent mess focused entirely on trying to get through the next twenty-four hours.

I arrive home to be swamped with hugs from the boys. I do my utmost to play with them and make up for my three-week absence.

The day drags by slowly. I try to eat something, but the nerves for tonight's show snuff out any glimmer of an appetite. I try to sleep—unsuccessfully.

Eventually it's time to go to the theatre. I leave Annie to sort out the babysitting issues, and I drive the car in to work. She'll follow soon after in a cab.

As I work my way through the twilight traffic, I spot the theatre across Darling Harbour, lit by the sunset. Seeing it from a distance so objectively reminds me that outsiders still have no concept of what to expect, or what we've all been through to put the show on stage. To them it's still just an idea waiting to hit the world.

It's taken an army of creative people toiling under enormous pressure to get it up. Creative blocks, technical disasters and deadlines, which have squeezed people to breaking point, have all taken their toll, none of which will be apparent when the curtain rises in an hour and half. Tonight is the culmination of so many elements of this endeavour. This is one of the most anticipated Australian musicals ever, and for me personally, it marks my return to big musical theatre. I want to dazzle my detractors and reward those who fought for me. I want to honour the strange and sometimes chaotic journey I've been on to get here.

When I arrive at the theatre, the nervous energy is palpable. Even though we've already done the show seven times, it feels like it's our first. The tempo is ferocious. People scurry all around me. I feel like I'm walking in slow motion as my energy is low and I'm still crook as a dog.

I wander into Tony's dressing room, which is filled to the brim with cards, flowers and gifts. He looks up at me, beams, and asks how I am. 'Not bad,' is the best I can muster, and we share a look that to both of us reads: Well, we're finally here.

I pass him an opening night card, one of two I've bought. The other is for Daniel. He thanks me generously and says, 'Chookas.'

I head into my own dressing room and find it is also filled to the brim with gifts, cards and flowers. My heart sinks. I knew this would be the case, and I'm filled with remorse that, besides my two closest cast members, I haven't got anyone else a single thing. I curse my illness for depriving me of so many delicious moments leading up to tonight, one of which is the delivering of gifts on opening night.

I close my dressing room door, half in shame, and begin sifting through the incredibly generous collection of good wishes. I open cards, speed reading the kind words so many of the cast and crew have spent valuable time composing. I become emotional because I feel so left out. None of this love has been reciprocated.

There's a tap at the door. Trevor pops his head in.

'Hi, daaarling,' he sings. 'How are you feeling?' I tell him I'm not great, but I'll be all right. He passes me a phone number written on a piece of scrap paper. 'Stephan Elliott wants you to call him.'

Intrigued, I immediately dial the number. He's already in the bar and obviously drinking away his nerves. He tells me he loves what I'm doing in the show and to not change a thing. My performance has heart and integrity and truth. I'm bowled over. Being a performer so often consists of feeling like a fake—that at any moment the audience, or anyone else for that matter, will work out that you're just a phoney. Jill Perryman, one of Australia's greatest performers, who played Dolly Levi in *Hello, Dolly!* used to have a catch cry almost every night when we finished our bows. She'd turn to us and say, 'Fooled them again!' So to hear such encouragement from Stephan half an hour before going on stage is music to my ears. I thank him profusely and hang up. I decide then and there to take all the love that I've been offered over the last fifteen minutes from the cards, the flowers, the gifts, the bottles of wine and from Stephan, and draw it all up into the inspiration that will get me through the show tonight.

I do my make-up with an unsteady hand, trying to ward off my nerves. I breathe even breaths. I try to visualise my performance coming to me effortlessly. And then suddenly there I am, standing side stage with my fishnets and my corset under my overcoat, ready to walk on stage.

Every luminary, celebrity and would-be celebrity in Sydney has been invited. Most have shown up and are now sitting expectantly in the house, along with friends, family, nervous producers and cunning, ticket-scrounging fans of the movie. Rumours of the nightmare build-up to tonight are bound to have leaked far and wide, and many, I'm sure, are anticipating the worst. While we've been fighting anxiety and wrestling with our confidence backstage, they've been arriving and strutting the red carpet, smiling at the snapping press and giving out air kisses nineteen to the dozen. To most of them, this is all just a glamorous photo opportunity, and they haven't got a clue what to expect. But then again, we don't either. What we're about to do is a high-wire act. No one can predict if the bus will work. We haven't had a single run of the show without stopping, and we haven't had a dress rehearsal. The sense of good humoured 'take it as it comes' relaxation that I manufactured in the previews has left me, and all I want is a streamlined performance, which is slick and professional. Tonight I don't have the stomach to be humiliated.

As the beginning of the show approaches, good luck hugs are tossed about with gay abandon. Everyone finds that special person or persons to squeeze one last time before they leap into the breach.

I seek out Tony, Dan and Marney. We're all shitting ourselves, but we sport a kind of excited, brave face over the top of it. It's particularly meaningful for Tony and me, being the only ones who have ridden this beast from the very beginning.

'Be beautiful,' he says, and struts back towards his dressing room. I now disengage from the rest of the cast and take a moment to myself. I draw up all the concentration I can muster, tell myself to ignore the sore throat, the cough, the aching joints and the exhaustion, and just get through this one last show. The honest truth is that I shouldn't be here at all. If I worked in a bank I'd be home, tucked up in bed with a hot water bottle and half a jar of Vicks smeared across my chest. But this is the theatre. Different rules apply, and come eleven o'clock it will all be finished and done.

The overture begins. A surge of nerves washes through the company, and a steely focus sets in everybody's eyes. The curtain rises, and the crowd instantly applauds the sight of the illuminated Sydney Harbour Bridge. Then the Divas descend from the heavens singing 'Downtown'. This brings the roof down, and the first eight bars of the song are completely inaudible. Dancers hit the stage and the routine begins. My cue approaches, and my nerves turn to dread. 'Don't fuck this up, don't fuck this up.' I push through the flitter curtain and make my entrance, steadying myself as I go. My head pounds with adrenalin, and I work hard to concentrate on my performance and not my nerves. The song goes well. I make my on-stage change and then head off to finish the rest off stage. The song ends and the audience roars. Next up is 'Never Been To Me'. I race to my moving platform and stand waiting to be shoved on stage. I strike my pose and before I know it I make my debut as a drag. My legs are shaking beneath my dress, and I hope to God no one notices. As I run off from performing the song, I feel a sense of relief, like I've left a good proportion of my nerves back there in the song. I make my change into the funeral, feeling slightly more relaxed. This is the kind of curve I want to be on.

By the end of the show I don't want a single thread of anxiety left in my body.

The show runs more smoothly than it ever has. We don't need to stop once. The jokes seem to fire, and the dramatic moments feel like they're hitting their marks. When I feel uncertain of how I'm going, I remind myself of Stephan's words.

By the end of the first act, my energy is waning. My voice feels hoarse from all the coughing, and I'm not confident at all singing the gentle stuff. I find myself retreating into an idle whenever the focus is not on me, just to conserve what little energy I've got left. Although I feel like I'm going okay, I'm struggling to match the enormous energy that Tony is belting out. He owns every part of his performance, and he squarely connects it with the audience. Dan is going really well too. He's so well cast for the part, and he oozes sexuality through the entire show, winning hearts as he goes.

Tick is a hard role to place. Bernadette and Felicia have all the jokes and the flashy moments, while Tick has all the secrets and the drama. My job is to resist the temptation to join in their party, and instead to offer a different dynamic. It's a much subtler performance, and one I hope captures the audience's hearts and imagination.

After 'Always On My Mind' I lead my son off stage and through a doorway in the flitter curtain. Last night when I reached this moment we both ran straight into a flat, which blocked our way. We bounced backwards with the force. I had understood that this was my path to my next quick change behind the bus, which would then get me onto the lift and up to the top of Uluru. After last night's accident I've assumed they've changed my path without telling me, so tonight we run straight off stage into the side wings. I rip off my clothes so I'm wearing nothing but stockings, and I bolt for the back of the bus. But last night's version was wrong, so by the time I get to the back of the bus there's no flat there to conceal me from the audience when I run from the wings. The lift cue is fast approaching, and there's no alternative but to race, nude, bar a pair of stockings, in full view of the audience and across the stage to the back of the bus. I inhale a deep breath and take the plunge. Troy is in fits of laughter and asks what the hell I'm doing. The change is too quick to explain, but I hope dearly no one saw the strange little naked flash streak across the stage.

We reach the finale. Tony, Dan, and I swap relieved glances as we mount the scissor lift in our Opera House costumes. By the time we reach the pinnacle of the lift, I see that the audience is already on its feet. We haven't even finished the show, and they're giving us a standing ovation. For the first time tonight, I breathe deeply. I couldn't be happier. I've had some rotten old opening nights where the audience has just hated the show, and it's a terrible feeling. Tonight, beyond a shadow of a doubt, they have loved it.

As we head down to take our bows the volume of the cheering is overwhelming. It's like a rock concert. We stand for what seems like ten minutes taking it all in. I hunt through the crowd for Annie's face and find her beaming up at me. I wave to her, and she blows me a kiss.

When the curtain finally falls, the company collapses into each other's arms as if we've just presided over a successful lunar landing. Simon has come up on stage for the bows and is pumping with excitement. I hug him and whisper in his ear, 'We did it!' and we share a moment's celebration together.

The excited love fest soon disperses, and everyone heads off to get beautiful for the party. I shower and change into the D&G suit Fernando wrangled me, still wondering how much it will cost, and head off to the party at the casino showroom.

I arrive to a solid mass of people and thumping music. As I push through the crowd, I'm slapped on the back and complimented as I go, but there's only one opinion

I'm interested in. Annie is somewhere in the crowd, and all I want is to find her. At first I fear I never will, as the crowd is so huge and densely packed, but then halfway to the front I see her nursing a glass of champagne and chatting. I rush over and we embrace.

'That was fantastic,' she says. I can tell she means it, and I now feel like I can relax. I resolve to drink two glasses of red and then disappear.

The atmosphere is charged and strangely anonymous. Annie and I prowl the room to try and connect with the cast, but it's hard to find anyone. Usual practice for an opening night party is for the producers to get the cast up on stage and introduce them one by one. This has been abandoned for some reason, and it makes for a very disconnected mood. There's no focus to the party at all.

I hook up with my agent, Lisa, and we have a yack. I meet Barry Humphries, which is a huge thrill. I do a post-mortem with Liz, one of the producers, but before long, the exhaustion overtakes the adrenalin, and I ache to go home.

Annie and I slip out of the party and head back to Coogee. For the first time in three weeks we lie in bed and talk. We deconstruct the show, talk about what works, where it falls short and what needs to improve. She tells me what she and the kids have been up to, and for a good three hours I feel like a real person again. Before we know it, it's 5.00 am and the kids will soon be up. I don't care. The monkey is off my back. I can fall down dead and the world will still turn. Opening night is over.

Chapter 20
Year of the Queen

Usually when a show opens, the creative team's job is pretty much done and they exit, stage left. The exodus of the creative team on this show is like a scramble of shoppers hitting a Boxing Day sale, but played in reverse.

Our Sunday matinee is devoid of a single member of the creative team—a lonely feeling. All these fabulous guardians who've been working tirelessly to help get the show up have upped and left us en masse.

I positively limp through the show, having no voice left and being bereft of any energy reserve. As I drive home afterwards, I feel incredibly excited by the prospect of a day off.

School holidays finished a week ago, so Annie and the kids are due to head back to Melbourne tomorrow to get Hunter to school.

We spend our last night together rolling our eyes at how little we've actually seen each other these last three weeks. I'm secretly relieved I'm going to get some quality sleep in their absence. Hopefully, I'll be able to shake off this bitch of a flu.

On Monday morning the reviews appear and at best can be described as mixed. My jaw drops as I read them. Were these guys at the same show? Not a note of the genuine screaming, stomping standing ovation we saw at the end of the show made it into any of the reviews. Bewildered, I read them over and over. One of them even suggests the producers lacked imagination because they couldn't come up with a better name for the show. Not being that aware of Sydney reviewers, this comment alone gives me an insight into their worth. *What the hell else would you call it?*

My mother-in-law sends me a review from an Auckland paper, which raves about the show and makes a point of calling the Sydney reviewers snobs for their cool take on the show.

I drop the family at the airport on Monday afternoon. I feel empty having to say goodbye to them again, but cheer myself with the thought that between now and when I have to be in at the theatre on Tuesday night I won't get out of bed.

Still wracked with guilt from not having given a single thing to any of the cast for opening night, I begin to concoct ways to make it up to them. I consider wine and flowers and personalised gifts, but all this requires me getting out of my sickbed. A brilliant idea strikes me. I'll get them a male stripper.

Besides me, there are only four other straight guys in the cast, and even they'll appreciate the fun of it. I get on the phone and call the number from the biggest ad in the Yellow Pages. I speak to a gangster who takes my details, making it sound like he's writing them on a napkin. I ask him several times if he's sure he's got everything, and he gets snappish with me. 'Yeah, yeah, mate, she's sweet.' I request a fireman, and for extra cash I ask that he goes all the way. I compose a poem for him to read, which explains that I was too sick to get them anything last week, and that this is to make it up to them for my lack of opening night love.

Tuesday night rolls around, and I practically shake with nerves and excitement as seven o'clock approaches and I have to meet the stripper. I've organised with Kath that she call a company meeting for the entire cast and crew in the rehearsal room, so there's no chance anyone will miss out. I shepherd the stripper to a hidden dressing room, where he changes into his fireman's outfit. When everyone's assembled in the rehearsal room I lead him in. His costume is so convincing that everyone thinks he's a real fireman, and they've all been assembled for a drill.

He's pretty hot, so he quickly gets everyone's attention. Then he reads out the poem. Confusion spreads across the assembled faces. 'What the?' As the poem progresses, people begin to catch on. Anticipation mounts in the room until he finally hits play on his CD player and begins his strip.

The room erupts into thirteen-year-old girls at a pop concert squeals. The stripper takes various females from the audience and gets them to remove items of his costume, but this isn't what the cast want to see. They want one of the boys up there. It takes the stripper some time to work this out, but when he eventually does the room goes completely wild. This is the perfect way to begin the week. The show is still crawling on its way to learning how to walk, and we're all still exhausted from our marathon build up, but this event sends everyone on their way feeling joyful and eager to get into it once more. I feel happy I've given them something back.

In a strange way the work had really just begun. For the next three weeks we did what we should have been doing in previews: examining our performances, listening to the audience, working the jokes, honing the scenes, and testing the pacing. It was an exciting time because you could feel the show getting stronger and starting to swing.

Just as we were beginning to feel we were on solid ground, Dan had an unfortunate incident and broke two bones in his hand. This immediately put him out of the show for six weeks, and Nick Hardcastle was forced to step in and take over. In a show like this, it takes several weeks, even months, to train up an understudy. At this point, none of the three leads' understudies were officially ready, so the shock of Dan having to go was intense.

Luckily, Nick had been involved early on and had been doing his homework. He stepped into the fray one Saturday matinee and quite literally saved the show. Without completely knowing the lines and never having rehearsed some of the scenes before, he made it through with pure determination and tenacity, and he distinguished himself as being a remarkable performer by delivering one of the most incredible feats I've ever seen by an understudy.

Ross disappeared from the show completely, leaving us with the legacy of a bunch of fabulous routines, drilled with military precision by Mark, our dance captain.

Simon returned for a few whirlwind trips with the promise of tightening the show in the future and implementing re-writes of some of the scenes. As the season progressed, I became aware that Tick was lacking not only in jokes but also in substance, and I began to lobby for more of both. Simon assured me that he was aware of this, and that it would eventually happen.

Spud made a few appearances to give notes and to tighten the odd piece of music. A couple of muted notes of praise from him made me feel he was pleased with where I'd finally got to vocally.

The show seemed to attract celebrities on a regular basis. Sir Elton John watched one night and came backstage for a photo opportunity and to tell us how much he loved it. I almost missed meeting him altogether as I was busting for a piss when the curtain fell. I raced back to my dressing room to unburden myself, but of course it was the piss that would never end. I could hear Kath tentatively calling me from the corridor, 'Jeremy, he's here. Are you coming?'

'I'm coming, I'm coming!' I yelled, desperately trying to choke it off.

Hugo Weaving came as well. Having him watch the show was nerve wracking, but it was a real thrill to meet him and to chat about the show and the role.

Nick Hardcastle's six weeks in the role took us up to Christmas, which for me marked a whole year of being a part of the show—the end of the year of the queen. In the very same week as last year, the week before Christmas, I found myself composing a eulogy for another dear friend who had just died. The year of the queen tragically bookended by two funerals. I successfully applied to the company to have a night off so I could attend the funeral in Melbourne. Now I was confronted with the strangest feeling. Giving the role over to my understudy—a role I had created, a role I'd invested so much of myself in, and now I was handing it over to someone else to play—felt like I was pushing a little paper boat out onto a lake.

As I left Sydney, I had an empty feeling. I'd only be one night away and tomorrow I'd be back on stage again—and would be, it seemed, for the foreseeable future. But what I was actually doing was forever relinquishing the exclusivity of being Tick. I was happy to share Tick with my capable understudy, David, but somehow, it felt like the end.

Funny old year, huh?

Post Script

Priscilla went on to perform for eleven months in Sydney and then travelled to Melbourne to the Regent Theatre for another nine months. By then it was the top grossing Australian musical in history.

It then moved to New Zealand and enjoyed a sold out six week season in Auckland. This is where I left the show. Around seven hundred performances later it was time to hang up the stilettos and hand the reins over to a new Tick.

The show returned to Sydney for a short season before opening in London, Toronto, New York, Milan and Brazil. It remains the most successful Australian show of all time, and it's a credit to the vision and tenacity of a group of exceptional people: Stephan Elliot, Simon Phillips, Ross Coleman, Garry McQuinn, and Spud Murphy.

Let's hope *Priscilla* keeps shaking her groove thang for many years to come.

The Original Cast

Bernadette - Tony Sheldon
Tick - Jeremy Stanford
Felicia - Daniel Scott
Bob - Michael Caton
Shirl - Genevieve Lemon
Marion – Marney McQueen
Cynthia - Lena Cruz
Miss Understanding - Trevor Ashley
Diva - Danielle Barnes
Diva - Sophie Carter
Diva - Amelia Cormack
Jimmy - Kirk Page
Frank - Ben Lewis
Bernadette Understudy & Ensemble - Rohan Senior
Tick Understudy & Ensemble - David Spencer
Felicia Understudy & Ensemble - Nick Hardcastle
Bob Understudy & Ensemble - Damien Bermingham
Dance Captain & Ensemble - Mark Hodge
Ensemble - Michael Griffiths
Ensemble - Kurt Phelan
Ensemble - Damien Ross
Ensemble - Dean Vince
Swing - Jeremy Youett
Swing - Christina O'Neill
Swing - Sean McGrath
Benji - Joshua Arkey
Benji - Alec Epsimos
Benji - Rowan Scott
Benji - Joel Slater

The Creative Team

Director - Simon Phillips
Writers - Stephan Elliott and Allan Scott
Choreographer - Ross Coleman
Musical Arranger, Director and Supervisor –
Stephen "Spud" Murphy
Set Designer - Brian Thomson
Costume Designers - Tim Chappel and Lizzy Gardiner
Lighting Designer - Nick Schlieper
Sound Designer - Michael Waters

The Producers

Back Row Productions – Liz Koops and Garry McQuinn,
Specific Films – Michael Hamlyn,
Allan Scott,
John Frost,
and Michael Chugg
in association with MGM On Stage.

About the Author

Jeremy Stanford has been a performer for over thirty years. His break out performance was playing Buddy in *The Buddy Holly Story*. His other credits in musicals include *High Society, Hello, Dolly!, Sweet Charity, Company, Looking Through A Glass Onion, South Pacific,* and *Light in the Piazza*. On stage he's worked for the MTC, Playbox, STC, and Handspan, and on TV he's performed in many Australian TV staples such as *The Doctor Blake Mysteries, Jack Irish, Winners and Losers,* and *Wentworth*. In 2013 he completed his first feature film, *The Sunset Six*, which he directed, co-wrote and co-produced. Since then he has directed stage productions of *Rent* and *Into the Woods,* as well as directing his first operas, *Dr Miracle,* and *First the Music, Then the Words*. In 2018 Jeremy will release his debut novel *Rapture*. He lives in St Kilda with his wife and two sons.

Acknowledgements

Thanks to Garry McQuinn for being so unbelievably helpful. More a buddy than a producer—and thanks for the cover shot. Thanks to Tim Chappel and Lizzy Gardiner for the faaaabulous outfit for the cover. To Troy Armstrong and Sophie Hamley for great advice. Lisa Mann and Carol Raby for your steadfast belief. Simon Phillips for absolutely everything but most of all your faith. To Lou Ryan for convincing me it was a good idea to write this book in the first place and for all your invaluable help. To Steve Worland for getting the ball rolling. Thanks to Anne-Marie Reeves for the cover design, David Spencer and Michael Caton for the rehearsal pics and to Tony Sheldon and Genevieve Lemon for their tweaking suggestions. Kathryn Moore came in to do a final edit of this edition and, of course, worked her usual magic on it. To Mum for the oceans of love. And to my incredible wife, Annie. This couldn't have happened without you. You're amazing.

CPSIA information can be obtained
at www.ICGtesting.com
Printed in the USA
LVHW020351140420
653367LV00002B/404

9 780994 439987